SEEING IS BELIEVING

Frances and Malcolm Chance, the retired head-master of a minor public school, now live quietly in the village of Raneswood in well-deserved and long-awaited peace. However, this rural tran-quillity is rudely shattered when their next-door neighbour, Peter Loxley, is shot to death in his own home while his wife Avril is in London.

At first suspicion falls automatically on Fred Dyer, the red-haired local handyman, who was not only seen entering the Loxley house, but has also been suspected of three sex crimes in another village. Dyer provides an alibi, however, and the case against him begins to look distinctly weaker, especially with the possibility that the killer was wearing a red wig.

When it is discovered that Avril's marriage was floundering and that Avril herself was the object of another man's desires, it looks as though those with a motive for murder are almost as numerous as the passions that have been seething under the surface of an outwardly calm village life.

Seeing Is Believing

E · X · Ferrars

DOUBLEDAY

New York   London   Toronto   Sydney   Auckland

PUBLISHED BY DOUBLEDAY
a division of Bantam Doubleday Dell Publishing Group, Inc.
1540 Broadway, New York, New York 10036

DOUBLEDAY and the portrayal of an anchor with a dolphin are
trademarks of Doubleday, a division of Bantam Doubleday Dell
Publishing Group, Inc.

Library of Congress Cataloging-in-Publication Data

Ferrars, E. X.
Seeing is believing / E.X. Ferrars.—1st ed.
p. cm.
I. Title.
PR6003.R458S4   1996
823'.912—dc20   95-13270
CIP

448 0006
ISBN 0-385-47543-8

Printed in the United States of America
January 1996
First Edition in the United States of America

1 3 5 7 9 10 8 6 4 2

Seeing Is Believing

CHAPTER 1

When Malcolm Chance, my husband, retired at the age of seventy, from being headmaster of Granborough, a co-educational, slightly freakish school in the village of Bolding, near to the little town of Edgewater, we had to make up our minds where we would like to settle. Not that we had not been discussing this for the last few years. We knew that we should have to leave the Headmaster's House, where we had lived comfortably for the last ten years, and were torn between a desire to remain in some other house in Bolding, where, after all, we should be amongst most of our friends, and the thought that it would be best to move some considerable distance away, the advantages of which would be that Malcolm need not be continually troubled by seeing the changes that his successor was sure to be making in the running of the school, and that it would really be fairer to him if Malcolm was not close at hand to cast his shadow over him.

The fact that his successor was going to be Brian Hewlett, who had been second master almost as long as Malcolm had been headmaster, and who was a close friend, did not affect our feelings; in fact, in some ways it only made the argument stronger for moving well out of Brian's way, and in the end this was what we decided to do. We bought a pleasant old house in the village of Raneswood, about sixty miles from Edgewater, and after the expected festivities in the way of dinners and presentations that had occurred on our departure among children and staff, we said goodbye to them all and moved away.

It was more painful to go than either of us had honestly anticipated, but our house and Raneswood had been a lucky choice. The village was small enough for its activities to have remained intimate in character, and we found ourselves welcomed into them with a pleasant friendliness. Malcolm soon made his mark, in spite of his age, in the cricket eleven, and in helping to organize the village Produce Association; while I became involved in local dramatics. It was on account of the dramatics that Avril Loxley came to see me one Friday morning, bringing with her, it need not be said, her three dogs: a black, curly-haired retriever, a Labrador and a Belgian shepherd, without which I had very seldom seen her. Though they were all rather large dogs, they were well-trained and by then were used to me and my house, so that although they seemed to take up a considerable amount of space in our sitting room, they were not really much in the way, when Avril got to work, trying on my costume as Juliet's nurse, in the modern dress production of *Romeo and Juliet* that we should shortly be presenting in the village hall.

We were rather proud of ourselves for having ventured on modern dress. It made us feel progressive and intellectual, but since we had, I could not really understand why I need not wear one of my everyday dresses. But Avril had insisted that I must be dressed like a real nanny of the upper classes, and being a clever dressmaker, with not enough to do to fill her time, she was enjoying running up a pale blue cotton dress for me, and making me a rather fanciful little cap. There was a large quantity of theatrical gear of all kinds in a cupboard in the village hall, left over from earlier productions, for we were a very active group, and Avril was in charge of these, but this time they would not be needed except for a few things such as rapiers and a lute or two. But she managed to keep pretty busy, inducing us to exchange clothes with one another whenever she thought the characters required this, and so succeeding in keeping nearly as fully occupied as she would have been if we had been producing the play in full Elizabethan grandeur.

'I'm going to London tomorrow,' she remarked, crouching at my feet as she pinned up the hem of my blue cotton dress. 'I'm having lunch with my cousin, Lynne Denison. You know she's my cousin, do you?'

She looked up at me questioningly as she said it. Of course I knew it. The whole village knew it. Ever since Lynne Denison had been awarded an Oscar for her performance in *Dark Shadows*, a particularly gruesome murder story, we would have had no chance of escaping knowledge of the relationship. Like her cousin, Avril had started a career in films, but either had not had the talent, or the dogged capacity for hard work that would have been necessary for even modest success, and had given it up in favour of marriage.

She was quite as good-looking as her cousin; tall, slender, and with a natural grace in all her movements, fair hair that she drew back almost austerely from her oval face, wide-spaced blue eyes, and delicate features. She was thirty-five and married to a man about seven years her junior, but seeing them together, this would not have occurred to anyone. Peter Loxley was very good-looking too, in a dark, muscular, slightly formidable way which tends to look older than it should in youth, but not so very much older twenty years later. He was a junior partner in the publishing firm of Loxley Matthews, which had been founded by his father, from whom he had inherited the dignified old Queen Anne house in which he and Avril lived. They were our next-door neighbours.

Perhaps at this point I should say a few things about myself. I was sixty-seven at the time of which I am writing: small, weighed eight and a half stone, had hair that had once been dark and curly, but had long ago gone grey, and as it had turned grey it had also rather

9

mysteriously lost its curliness and become almost straight. I wore it cropped short, which I had never thought of doing while it waved about my ears and forehead. I have a square sort of face, dark eyes and undistinguished features.

I had begun life as a nurse, which perhaps made my part in our production of *Romeo and Juliet* most appropriate, though I seldom thought about those early days now, as I had been married to Malcolm for nearly forty years. He had been teaching in a conventional public school when we first met, and it had never occurred to me then that I should end up as the wife of a headmaster, and of a place like Granborough. I had never tried to be a headmistress, but I had always been a good deal involved in the life of the school, and had had to entertain a fair amount because there had always been a steady stream of parents visiting the place, old Granborough pupils, and sometimes notabilities who happened to be interested in our ideas of education, or who came to give us lectures on sometimes very obscure subjects, or otherwise to entertain us. So I confess that for a time I found life in Raneswood rather quiet, but after a little while came to recognize that this suited me very well. I sometimes thought of the old life with nostalgia, but would not have gone back to it even if I had ever had any opportunity of doing so.

'So she's come over to England, has she?' I said, as Avril sat back on her heels, studying the hem of my dress and frowning slightly as if she were not quite satisfied with it. 'Is she staying long?'

Lynne Denison had lived in Hollywood for some years.

'She hasn't told me,' Avril answered. 'She arrived last weekend and we've only spoken on the telephone . . . No, I think it ought to be at least an inch longer. Just turn round, will you? I'll start again from this seam at the back.'

I was growing a little tired of standing still in the middle of the room, and thought that if only Avril would take a tape-measure to the job it would be finished in a few minutes, but she preferred to rely on her own eyes.

'How long is it since you last met?' I asked.

'About three years. In fact, I haven't seen her since she became really successful. I hope it hasn't changed her much. I always knew she was headed for success, of course, and when we were young I used to be furiously jealous of her. But she was too nice for me to keep it up. If she's staying long enough in England, I'm going to try to persuade her to come down here for our *Romeo and Juliet*. She might be able to help us quite a lot.'

'She won't do that,' I said. 'She's a professional, and if there's one thing that the professional actor or actress hates and despises, it's an amateur. And that isn't true only of stage people. Most real professionals in any line have no use at all for the amateur. Take scientists, and chefs, and writers, and politicians – oh, any kind of people where there's a real distinction between the ones who have learnt to work at the job for a living, as against the ones who only do it for fun.'

I felt a slight twinge of conscience as I said this, because a few weeks before, Malcolm had started to write his auto-biography. He had never yet written a book, though he had written enough lectures and papers to make one, and I thought it sure to be obviously the work of an amateur, like the autobiographies of so many elderly people who are afflicted by the desire to write about their lives in the days of retirement. If they have always been writers, the results may be interesting; but if they have merely been people of general talent and intellect, they are only too likely, however interesting their lives have been, to pro-duce something boring and flat. I had come across a number of such things, which had made me try to dis-suade Malcolm from attempting to write his life story, but as it happened, at that very moment he was upstairs in his little room that we called his study, working away at it.

11

'Well, I'm going to do my best to persuade her to take an interest in us,' Avril said, and looking down at her as she crawled round me, I recognized the stubborn expression on her face that I had often seen there. It could change her calm and gentle-looking face to something hard and determined. 'After all, a lot of her success has been luck. If she hadn't met Walt Denison when he was on the way up himself, she'd never have had her first chance.'

'Is she still married to him?' I said.

'Oh no, there've been two since then. I'm not sure what the situation is at the moment, but no doubt I shall hear tomorrow . . . There, I think that looks about right.' She stood up and took a step backwards to look at her handiwork. 'That's very nice, though I admit you may have been right that Juliet's nurse wouldn't have been wearing a uniform. After all, Juliet was fourteen, wasn't she – a bit young to be having a passionate love-affair, but a bit old to have a nurse.'

'When I was young myself,' I said, 'I used to think it was absurd that she should be so in love at her age and I thought that Elizabethans must have been very strange people, but times have changed recently and if you'd seen what I did at school, you wouldn't think there was anything strange about it. And the young Montagues and Capulets were just the kind of gangs who fight each other nowadays, though ours mostly have motorbikes.' I knew the idea was not original, but it pleased me. 'But at least they don't seem to have had trouble with drink and drugs.'

'Did you have trouble with drink and drugs at that school of yours?' Avril asked.

'A bit. Not much. Not nearly as much as there'd have been at an urban school.'

'I hope our Juliet isn't that way inclined. She seems so perfectly right for the part.'

12

'I think she's a pretty sober young thing, even if she's got a boyfriend.'

As it happened, the boyfriend was Romeo. There had been a faction in our dramatic society who had wanted Peter Loxley to be Romeo, but it was Fred Dyer who in the end had been given the part. Peter was Mercutio, while Avril was Lady Capulet. There were people in the society who felt uneasy about Fred. We really knew so little about him. He had simply appeared some months ago in the company of Sharon Sawyer, our Juliet, and made no attempt to conceal the fact that he was living with her.

They lived in the ground-floor flat of a house that had once been a vicarage, but which was much too large for the modest needs of our present vicar and had been converted into flats. Sharon worked in the library in Otterswell, our nearest small town and was a quiet, pretty girl who knew her Shakespeare so well that she had hardly needed to study her part. Nobody knew quite what Fred Dyer did, except that he would mend electric light fittings that had gone wrong, and paint doors and window-frames, and look after your garden if you were lucky, and wash your car. There was a story that he was a poet, though I was certain that he had never said so himself. Either Sharon had spread it, or someone had guessed it because there had to be some explanation of what he was really doing in a place like Raneswood. It did not seem improbable that a penniless poet should spend his spare time as an odd-job man and there was something pleasantly romantic about the idea. He had a black leather jacket and jeans, which was convenient, as it was how we had decided the young Montagues and Capulets should be dressed.

Avril stood up and began packing up her dressmaking tools, while I removed my blue nurse's dress and started scrambling into my slacks and sweater. Her dogs recognized this correctly as a sign that she was going home and got to their feet too, stretching, yawning, wagging their tails to show their satisfaction, and began wandering about the room, seeming all at once to fill it almost completely. It was not a large room, though usually I did not think of it as small, but when three big dogs took it into their heads to explore it yet again after having done so on arriving, it seemed to shrink in size. The house was really a cottage, but it was Georgian and the ceiling was fairly high, the fireplace elegant, the doorway not the kind which forces anyone entering to stoop if they do not want to risk giving their heads a knock, but for the moment it seemed to be all damp noses and lolling tongues, and into the midst of this came Malcolm, having apparently decided that he had spent enough of the morning on his autobiography.

'Ah, Avril,' he said, 'at work as usual. You aren't just leaving, are you? Have some sherry.'

'That'd be nice,' she said. 'Mrs Henderson always looks shocked if she sees me drinking alone at home. I always wait till she leaves before I help myself.'

Mrs Henderson was the Loxleys' daily help, a little angular woman of extreme efficiency, who came to them from nine to twelve six days a week, and the reason why Avril would have had to drink alone if she had returned now was that Peter not only went daily to London, but sometimes remained for several days at a time in a small flat that they had in Fulham. I thought that that was where he was staying at the moment.

Malcolm went to the corner cupboard where we kept our drinks and brought out sherry and glasses. He is a tall, spare man, taller, in fact, than he looks now, because he has acquired a slight, elderly stoop. His hair is grey, but still thick and stands up in a bristling way above a high forehead. His eyes are a cool, clear blue. His chin is square and firm and his mouth wide. His face in general is a kindly one, though it can become remarkably stern if his mood happens to be disapproving. The change in it can still sometimes take me by surprise. He was to be Friar

Lawrence in our production, so he was the one member of the cast who was going to be clothed in something taken from the store of fancy dress that belonged to the society.

'You'll be at Hugh's this evening, I expect,' he said as he brought Avril her sherry. 'Will Peter be there?'

Hugh Maskell was an acquaintance of ours in the village who was directing our production, and who had asked us over for drinks that evening.

'If he gets home in time,' Avril answered. 'He thought he would; but it depends on the traffic, doesn't it? It sometimes takes two hours to get here from London, specially on a Friday evening.'

The dogs had investigated Malcolm, had decided that he had a right to be there and had settled down again, though rather reluctantly, more or less where they had been before.

'How are you dressing Juliet?' Malcolm asked, as he poured out drinks for me and himself and settled down on the sofa under the window. 'I hope not in jeans or a mini-skirt.'

'Definitely not in jeans,' Avril said, 'but the question of the mini-skirt isn't quite decided. I rather like the idea myself. After all, the girl's got very good legs.'

'No,' Malcolm said positively. 'The mini-skirt's only a whim of the moment, and the fact is, according to my observation, it's permissible these days to wear skirts of any length you choose. It's not like it used to be a little while ago. I can remember when Frances gave away two perfectly good dresses to Oxfam simply because the hemline was in the wrong place. A year or two later, she'd have been glad to have them back, because the hem had moved again. But now that simply doesn't arise. So why not put Juliet into something long and graceful? She'll look far more charming in it.'

Frances, by the way, is my name.

'Of course we'll think about it,' Avril said. 'I expect

15

there'll be a good deal more discussion of such things on Saturday evening than we've had already. You'll be there, of course.'

Saturday evening was to be our first rehearsal in the village hall. Most of us would be reading our parts, and arguing a great deal, getting in each other's way and wasting time. But it was a phase that had to be gone through.

'Will you be back from London, Avril?' I asked, then explained to Malcolm, 'Avril's going to London to have lunch with her cousin, Lynne Denison.'

'Oh yes, I'll come straight back after lunch,' Avril said. 'And of course, Peter'll be there.'

'Our problem is that we're expecting a guest for the weekend,' Malcolm said. 'We're going into Otterswell to meet him this afternoon. And we'll either have to bring him to the rehearsal, which might bore him, or leave him to himself for the evening.'

'Is he the kind of person who'd be bored by the rehearsal?' Avril asked. 'I should have thought it might be quite entertaining.'

'I think so too,' I said. 'After all, he's had quite a lot to do with amateur dramatics himself in the last few years. I think he'll enjoy it.'

But I was wrong. He did not enjoy it because it did not take place.

Something happened on Saturday that put an end to our production of *Romeo and Juliet*. So perhaps it was as well that it was to have been a modern dress production, because at least our society had so far spent hardly anything on the clothes. The material for my nurse's uniform was the only thing that had been bought with our rather scanty funds.

The guest whom Malcolm and I were expecting that afternoon was Brian Hewlett, now headmaster of Granborough. He had been to stay with us several times before during the school holidays. At the moment, we were in the middle of the spring holidays and we were hoping the fine weather that we were having would last over his visit, because he and Malcolm enjoyed going on long walks together over the Downs. I usually let them go without me, because generally Brian's wife Judy came with him, and she and I enjoyed each other's company. She was ten years younger than I was but that had never been a barrier. He was coming alone this time because she was on a visit to a member of her family whom she felt obliged to see from time to time, but whom she preferred not to inflict on Brian. Over the years, I had heard a good deal about her family, all of whom thought of Granborough as nothing but a deplorably eccentric institution and Brian as more than a little mad.

We were to meet him at three-forty-five in Otterswell. It was at about a quarter-past three that we went out to the garage and brought out the Rover. It was looking spruce, because Fred Dyer had recently washed it. As we went towards it, I saw him at work in the Loxleys' garden. He noticed us and gave us a wave. He was a tall young man, bony but muscular, with wide shoulders and long arms, and a small, well-shaped head set on a long neck with a pronounced Adam's apple. His hair was a deep, burnished red and his eyes were a greenish grey. In his gangling way he was striking to look at, if not exactly handsome, and although up to a point he was friendly, it was sometimes difficult to feel sure that he knew to whom he was talking. He seemed to look through you rather than at you, and to want to make sure that you realized that he liked to keep himself to himself. We had all been a little surprised when he had agreed to take the part of Romeo, indeed to have anything to do with our dramatic society. His girlfriend, Sharon, we supposed, must have been responsible for it. He was mowing the Loxleys' grass when we came out of the house.

While Malcolm was backing the car out of the garage,

17

I went across our own lawn and called out, 'Hello, Fred, when are you going to give us some time?'

He switched off the mower and came towards me. A low beech hedge divided the Loxleys' garden from ours and we could easily talk across it. Both gardens had several apple trees in them, and flowerbeds which at that time were making a brave show of tulips. The daffodils were over and so was the forsythia, and the rhododendrons were not yet in bloom. Our garden was a little the more ambitious, because Malcolm spent a good deal of time at work in it, so we were not quite as dependent on Fred as the Loxleys were. Our two houses stood close together, with only the hedge between them and paths going round to the back of each house. Our house was white, with dark beams and square sash windows, but the Loxleys' was a good deal bigger. I found its mellowed red brick and tall windows very attractive.

'I'll come over on Monday, if that's all right,' Fred answered. 'I'm busy over the weekend.'

He had a puzzling voice. Usually with the English, the moment they open their mouths you can place them socially, but Fred's accent eluded me. I thought there had probably been a public school at some time in his life, but if so, he had done his best to eliminate any trace of it. His busyness, I thought, was probably simply that he wanted to spend the weekend with Sharon.

'Monday's fine,' I said. 'Morning or afternoon?'

'I could come around ten.' As usual, he was not speaking directly to me, but seemed to be focusing on something beyond me, and I wondered if that was how he looked even at Sharon, because there was something a little chilling about it. 'Or shall I come earlier?'

'No, ten's all right, if that's what suits you.' I am not good at getting up myself, and was quite glad that he would not need attention earlier. Not that he needed much attention. He would arrive with his own tools in his van, which he would park at our gate, as it was parked

18

now at the Loxleys', and get to work with what he considered needed doing, without consulting Malcolm or me. Then, at about eleven o'clock, I would take him out a cup of tea, and we would have a brief chat, mostly about all the mistakes that we had made in our garden before he had come to our rescue and a little bit about the character of Romeo, then at twelve o'clock Malcolm would make out a substantial cheque to him, and he would drive off in his van. If he charged everyone he worked for as much as he charged us, he must have taken a comfortable income home to Sharon.

Malcolm by now had the car in the lane and I went to join him while Fred returned to the mowing-machine. The lane went down a fairly steep hill to the main road that ran through the village. There were three other houses along the lane, one of them belonging to Hugh Maskell to which we were going for drinks that evening, one to two elderly unmarried sisters, and one to a young couple called Askew with two small children. Hugh had been a highly successful surgeon before his retirement. He was sixty, which perhaps had been early to put an end to his career, but he claimed that he did not trust his hands any longer. Besides directing our performance of *Romeo and Juliet*, he was taking the part of Capulet.

The afternoon was fine, with a light breeze blowing and small puffs of cloud chasing each other across the clear blue sky. The hawthorn hedges were green and the beech trees were coming into leaf. It was only seven miles from Raneswood to Otterswell, along a twisting road that ran through two or three more villages. Brian was coming from Edgewater by train, which in fact had meant his going to London first and changing there, because Judy had taken their car when she went off to visit her family in Cheshire. We arrived at the station in Otterswell in plenty of time to meet the three-forty-five, and were waiting for Brian as arranged, at the bottom of the stairs that led up to the platform when the train came in.

Brian was among the first people who came down the stairs. He clapped a hand on Malcolm's shoulder and gave me a kiss. He was a small man, very neatly built, with a light, springing walk which seemed to make him move faster than anyone else around him. His hair was thick and grey and generally untidy; his face was narrow and long, with a pointed chin, a sharply jutting nose, a wide mouth, and large, very bright brown eyes. His fine, arched eyebrows were still black, in spite of his grey hair. He had never been handsome, yet he was a man whom one noticed in a crowd, mostly, I used to think, because he had so much vitality. He was carrying one suitcase which Malcolm tried to take from him but to which he clung, refusing to be helped with it. He seemed to think that our meeting was an occasion for chuckling rather than for speech, at least until we were in the Rover and on the way back to Raneswood.

Then he drew a deep breath, stretched comfortably in the seat beside Malcolm and said, 'Wonderful to be back here. You don't know how I've been looking forward to it. Peace and quiet. That's what you always give me here. Wonderful, it really is. Train was on time, too. That's wonderful these days. And I'm needing the peace and quiet more than usual. Life's been pretty hectic this last term.'

'Trouble?' Malcolm asked.

'No, not trouble. But the place is expanding and there's been a lot of planning to be done. You know, I'd like to be the headmaster of a really small school, the kind of place Granborough was fifty years ago. But I don't complain, at least not overmuch.'

'I hope it won't upset your ideas of peace and quiet that we're taking you out for drinks this evening,' I said from the back seat. 'If the thought appals you too much, we can leave you behind. We needn't stay long.'

'Dear me, no, that'll suit me nicely,' Brian said. 'All strange faces and no need to worry if you're going to say something that's going to give someone bitter offence. A touchy lot, schoolmasters and mistresses. Who's our host?'

'Someone I think you may have met on a previous visit,' Malcolm answered. 'His name's Hugh Maskell. He's a retired surgeon. He lives in the only modern house along our lane.'

'Maskell. Ah, yes. I remember him quite well,' Brian said. 'Remarkable thing the memory is, isn't it? He called in on you one day when Judy and I were staying with you a couple of years ago, and I think he stayed for about half an hour, yet I'd know him if we happened to meet casually in a London street. But expect me to recognize a parent who visited us only a week ago, and you'll find I'm floored. Most inconvenient. I'm in a job where, as you know, one's memory ought to be infallible.'

'How's Judy?' Malcolm asked.

'Annoyed,' Brian said. 'Definitely annoyed that I'm coming here when she'd committed herself to visiting that sister of hers. I'd be annoyed in her place too. Her sister is someone I can do without. I advise Judy to break the bond entirely, as really it means nothing to her, but she can't bring herself to do it and subjects herself to a week of irritation, boredom and pointless quarrelling at least once a year. There's no need to tell me blood's thicker than water. It certainly is, but I think I prefer water.'

Malcolm began to ask him questions then about some of the older members of the staff at Granborough, people whom we both remembered, whether they were still at the school or had moved on to higher things or retired. The drive home seemed short, and Fred Dyer was still at work when we drove past the Loxleys' gate. That is to say, he was just putting his tools away in his van and taking a broom out of it with which to sweep the paths, when he saw us and once again gave us a wave.

But the gesture was strangely, abruptly checked and he stared blankly at the car.

At the same moment, Brian said, 'Good God!'

21

Malcolm edged the car past the van and stopped at the entrance to our garage.

Brian repeated himself, 'Good God!' Then he went one further and muttered, 'Christ!'

'What's the matter?' I asked.

'That man,' Brian said. 'What's he doing here?'

'He does all kinds of things,' I said. 'Gardens, washed our car yesterday, puts new washers on taps if you need them, does minor electrical repairs. Oh, he's a treasure. Why, do you know him?'

'No!' Brian said with considerable violence. 'No – that's to say I don't *know* him. I may have exchanged a few words with him, but I could hardly help knowing who he is. You mean you don't?'

'We don't really know much about him,' I answered, 'except that he turned up here about four or five months ago as the boyfriend of one of the local glamour girls, and seems to live contentedly with her. There's a rumour around that he's a poet, but I don't think anyone's ever seen anything he's written.'

'What's his name?'

'Fred Dyer.'

'Well, that's something that it certainly is not.'

'What is it then?'

'When I last heard of him, he was called Jack Benyon.'

Brian and I had got out of the car and Malcolm was driving it into the garage. He took Brian's suitcase out of the boot, came out of the garage, locked it and started towards the house. But Brian stood still, looking towards the Loxleys' garden, where Fred Dyer's red hair was visible above the hedge.

'I could be mistaken,' Brian murmured. 'I suppose I could be.'

But he did not sound as if he believed that he was. Following Malcolm along the path to the house, he repeated thoughtfully, 'Benyon.' Then after a moment he added, 'That's the name he was using then. Don't expect it was any more his own than Dyer.'

'But when did you come in contact with him?' I asked.

We had reached our door and Malcolm had opened it.

'Did you never hear about the sex murders in Edgewater?' Brian said. 'There were three of them, all the same, and they've never been solved. But a man called Jack Benyon was nearly arrested for them.'

At his words, I felt a chill go through me, although I did not believe that his Jack Benyon and our Fred Dyer could possibly be the same person. But the mere thought of those murders in Edgewater a year ago was enough to make one shudder.

I led the way into the sitting room.

'I should think everyone in the country must have heard about them,' I said. 'Of course, we paid a bit of extra attention to them when the papers and television were full of them, knowing the place as we did.'

'But you said this man you're talking about was only nearly arrested for them,' Malcolm said. 'In other words, even if you're right that he's turned up here, he's innocent.'

'I don't think many people thought he was,' Brian said. 'But there wasn't enough evidence for a conviction. They took him in for questioning, but then they let him loose and he quietly disappeared. I know Detective Inspector Dalling quite well – he was in charge of the case – and he told me a bit more about it than perhaps he should have.'

'What was the evidence they had that made them suspect him?' Malcolm asked.

He had put Brian's suitcase down in our small hall, at the foot of the stairs, and was standing in the doorway of the room, ready to take Brian up to our spare bedroom. Brian was standing in front of the fireplace, where I had just switched on a bar of the electric fire that stood on the hearth. Though the spring day had been so bright, it was still cool and a little warmth was welcome.

'A woman saw him running away from the place where they later found a body,' Brian said. 'The third body. As you know, they'd all been killed in the same way: a black plastic rubbish bag pulled over the head from behind, then strangling. There wasn't any actual sexual assault, though her clothes were ripped and her body was bruised. Extreme sexual perversion, obviously, probably linked to impotence. And this woman who saw him running off described him perfectly. His red hair, his height, his thinness and all, and the clothes he was wearing. And she picked him out at once in an identity parade of red-haired men. Mostly men in red wigs, that's to say. They couldn't collect enough of the genuine article in Edgewater. But then she had second thoughts and said she was not at all sure that he was the man she saw, in fact she thought he wasn't. And the other bit of evidence was that Benyon, only the day before, had been into a hardware shop in Edgewater and bought a packet of those black rubbish bags, and when he was questioned about them one bag was missing, and he couldn't account for what he'd done with it. The girlfriend he had there said she'd taken it to line the dustbin, but as the rubbish people had just been round that day, there was no way of checking her story. She gave him an alibi too, which could have been true, though not many people believed it.'

'But that doesn't sound much like impotence,' Malcolm said. 'And I doubt if you could accuse our Fred of it, either.'

'How long was it after this girl saw the man, whoever he was, running away, that they found the body?' I asked.

'A couple of hours, I think,' Brian answered. 'It was dusk, which was partly why she wouldn't stick to her first story.'

'She didn't stop to investigate at the time?' I said.

'No. She didn't think much about it till she saw the

24

news of the murder on television that evening, then she got in touch with the police straight away. The television showed, you see, just where the body had been found, and she remembered at once what she'd seen.'

'Just where did that murder happen?' Malcolm said. 'It was somewhere down by the heath, wasn't it?'

There is a heath with a stream running through it on what used to be the edge of Edgewater, but in recent years buildings have slowly been creeping round it, so that it is losing its old, wild look. But there is still a good deal of gorse on it and as I remembered accounts of the murder, the body had been found in a patch of gorse.

Brian corroborated this.

'Yes, in some gorse. But they didn't think she'd been killed there, or at least not assaulted. They thought the object of the plastic bag was to prevent her being able to recognize the man if the murder somehow went wrong and she got away. Or it may have been less sensational than that, more some kind of fetishism. They never found that out, of course. There were no fingerprints on the bag.'

'What was the man Benyon doing in Edgewater?' Malcolm asked.

'Working in a garage,' Brian said. 'I used to take our car there to be serviced. That's why I told you I thought I'd exchanged a few words with him. I think I did. And it's why I recognized him at once when I saw him out there.' He nodded towards the window.

'He recognized you too,' I said. 'Anyone could see that. So perhaps Fred Dyer is Jack Benyon, even if he isn't necessarily a murderer. Now I think I'll get some tea.'

CHAPTER 2

The party that Hugh Maskell was giving was a small one. Besides ourselves there were only the Loxleys, Lucille Bird and her son Kevin, and Jane Kerwood. The Birds lived in the heart of the village in one of its few modern houses, designed by Kevin, who was an architect and who had designed Hugh Maskell's house. It was a white, square-looking place with a low-pitched roof of grey tiles, windows of great sheets of glass, a door approached from the garden by steep steps with no hand-rail which I was old enough to feel nervous of ascending in case I over-balanced, and at the back, a patio with a sculpture in one corner of it made of some kind of metal and which I believed, without being too sure about it, represented a nude woman.

Kevin was about thirty and the office in which he worked was in Otterswell. He was tall and slender, with a curiously wilted air about him, as if the burden of life was a bit too much for him. Perhaps the burden of living with Lucille would have been a bit much for anyone. Living up to her standards would always have been a strain. She expected almost everyone she met to be brilliant and successful, and if they did not quite achieve this, had a way of making them feel that they had intentionally failed her.

Kevin, unfortunately, was neither really brilliant nor successful, but only a moderately talented and hard-working young man, though very devoted to his mother. He had a pale, round face with large, somewhat protuberant dark eyes, a short nose, a small, rather tight-lipped mouth, soft, pink cheeks and a dimpled chin. His hair was dark and already growing scanty, so that his forehead looked very high, and with a few deep wrinkles across it, gave him a look of intellect which was a little misleading. He was not stupid, but he was not much interested in anything but reading the more bloodthirsty kind of thriller and in performing remarkable feats in the way of cookery. He was not easily amused and a reluctant chuckle was the nearest I had ever heard him get to laughter.

Lucille, who was sixty, had very little resemblance to her son. She was thin, sharp-featured and very erect. How long ago her husband had died I did not know for sure, but I had an idea that it was after only two or three years of marriage. She was a keen bridge player, worked hard in her garden and with considerable knowledge of what she was doing, so that it was about the most attractive in Raneswood. She drove a Mercedes with skill but slightly alarming aggressiveness, and seemed to be a rich woman, with her considerable wealth inherited, so I had heard, from various rich aunts and uncles. She had, I knew, some rich relations in Canada, whom she occasionally visited. In fact there was no need for Kevin to work for his living, but he probably did it, I thought, because it gave him a little independence. On the other hand, it might have been that Lucille would not have tolerated idleness. Sometime, sooner or later, she seemed determined he was to make his mark in the world. When he did, she would have the deep satisfaction of being the mother of a celebrity.

She was talking to Jane Kerwood when Hugh Maskell brought us into his drawing room. Hugh, who had known that we were bringing a friend, had recognized Brian at once.

'Mr Hewlett – of course – I'm afraid that name didn't mean anything to me when Malcolm asked if he might bring you with him – I'm hopelessly stupid at names,' Hugh said. 'Naturally, I said I'd be delighted, and how glad

I am that he suggested it, because I remembered quite clearly our very pleasant meeting a couple of years ago. But wasn't your wife with you then?'

Hugh was a tall, well-built man who looked less than his age, largely because he had kept the easy and supple way of moving of a much younger man. His light brown hair was only flecked with grey and though there were some deep lines on his face which at times gave it a grave, melancholic look, his skin was smoothly and healthily tanned. He had keen grey eyes under level eyebrows and strong, rather craggy features. When we first made his acquaintance, he had only recently lost his wife, who had died of leukaemia, which had been the real reason of his early retirement, as it had made him able to look after her through her long illness. There was no doubt that he had been tender and devoted, yet not long after her death he had shown signs of being interested in various women living in the village, and possibly some out of it too and it was the general view that he would remarry before very long.

Brian answered him, 'Yes, Judy was with me last time I came, but she's visiting her own family now.'

'And you live in Edgewater, don't you?' Hugh said. 'The place we've all heard so much about in recent times.'

Lucille heard him. 'Edgewater!' she cried in her thin, high voice. 'The place where they've had all those frightful murders! You really live there, do you? Do you know an awful lot about them?'

Hugh had not introduced Brian to her yet, but he did so now, and to Jane Kerwood, a small, pretty woman of about thirty who did not look as if she could be the Jane Kerwood who had ridden across the Sahara on a camel, seen some African civil wars at first hand, helped in famine and disease-stricken areas and written a very successful book about it all. But that was who she was, little though she ever spoke about it. She had soft, curly brown hair, gentle brown eyes, the most delicate of complexions, and

29

a generous mouth. As she was the nearest thing to a celebrity in the village, Lucille cultivated her with energy, which Jane appeared to mistake for the kindly interest of a wise, elderly woman in someone very young and ignorant. There had been several people in the dramatic society who had put forward the claim that she should be Juliet in our coming production, and it had only been her own insistence that she was too old for the part and that Sharon Sawyer would be far more suitable that had settled the matter. Actually, Jane had declined to take any part in the play.

While Hugh was bringing us our drinks, Lucille asked again, 'Do you know much about those murders, Mr Hewlett? After all, Edgewater's quite a small place, isn't it?'

'Small enough for almost nothing else to be talked about for some weeks,' Brian replied. 'But that didn't get them anywhere.'

'Wasn't anyone ever suspected?' Lucille asked.

'Oh, several people, I believe,' Brian said. 'But there was nothing conclusive.'

I was very relieved that he had decided against mentioning that one of the suspects worked in the Loxleys' garden and in ours, and sometimes, I believed, in Lucille's own, though most of the work in that was done by herself.

It was just then that the Loxleys arrived. As a matter of course they had brought their three dogs with them, since apparently they could not be left to themselves for an hour or two in an empty house, and the dogs had to be given the opportunity of investigating the drawing room and all of us who were in it before being turned out on to the patio, where they were safe enough from traffic because Hugh's garden was entirely enclosed by a high wooden fence. But they took their exclusion from the party in a bad spirit, barking and growling and rubbing their noses against the closed glass door that led out on to the patio, which Avril appeared to think was charming behaviour, and sure to please us all.

She stood at the door, her drink in her hand, saying, 'Be quiet, you naughty boys, be quiet!' Then she turned to smile at us, as if to make sure that we were enjoying the charm of the dogs' performance.

In a low voice to me, because I had sat down beside her, Lucille said, 'That woman ought to have had children. I wonder why she didn't.'

'Perhaps they just didn't happen,' I said.

'They might have adopted one or two then, mightn't they? But perhaps her husband was against it.'

Peter Loxley had given Jane and me each a kiss on entering, but had baulked at Lucille and now he was being introduced to Brian. His heavy, rather formidably handsome face was looking tired. There was an air of worry about him, which was not unusual. Though he was several years younger than Avril, it was unlikely that anyone would have guessed it, seeing them together. Perhaps it was all the travelling to London and back that he did that helped to tire him out, but I always felt that there were other strains upon him too. I was fairly sure that their marriage was not particularly successful.

Avril soon told everyone that she was going to London tomorrow to meet her cousin, Lynne Denison.

'I wonder if success will have changed her much,' she said. 'She used to be such a modest, quiet sort of person, who never made any show of her obvious talent. I want to persuade her to come down here to take a look at our *Romeo and Juliet*. Frances tells me of course she won't come, because there's nothing a professional hates like an amateur, but she was always so good-natured, I think she might come just to please us.'

'I don't see how she can help us,' Lucille said stiffly. She had not forgiven the society for not having chosen Kevin as Romeo, though he himself had shown no desire whatsoever to act. He was helping to make our scenery and showed a good deal of skill in this, and appeared to enjoy doing it, but to have no wish to take any part in the actual performance. 'If she'd arrived in time she might have been able to advise us on our casting. For instance, she might have been able to prevent our giving the part of Romeo to someone who doesn't even speak like an educated man. I've nothing against Fred Dyer, I like him very much, but in my humble opinion his accent is going to make him quite ridiculous.'

'It's said by some people,' Hugh said, 'that cockney is much nearer the way that Shakespeare himself would have spoken than our modern form of English.'

'Well, as we're doing the show in modern dress, I think we ought at least to do it in modern English too,' Lucille said sharply.

'Anyway, it isn't cockney that Fred speaks,' Avril said, 'and I think he's a pretty well-educated man. I think the chances are that he knows more about Shakespeare than any of us in this room.'

'I don't know if you've noticed it,' Kevin said, 'but when it's mentioned on television that the police want to interview a man who's just done a murder or robbed a bank, and they describe him in case any of us can help them to catch him, they never say that he has a cockney accent but always a London accent. There's a kind of inverted. snobbery about that, don't you think? The word cockney would apparently imply that he belonged to the working class, which would be improper.'

'Personally, I think the whole show is going to be a disaster,' Lucille said. 'Much too ambitious, in the first place.'

'But that's the fun of it,' Hugh said. 'And if we make fools of ourselves I don't think our audience will know it. They're liable to be a fairly simple-minded lot.'

'But if you advertised it more in Otterswell, as I'm sure you should,' Lucille went on complaining, 'and didn't rely just on the village, they might not be so simple-minded. I think you've approached the whole project in the wrong way.'

'Well, perhaps Lynne Denison will help us sort it out,' Peter said, but he said it wearily and it struck me that he would sooner be at home than brought out to this party. 'Avril's right, she's very good-natured.'

'But if you're going to London tomorrow, Avril,' Lucille said, 'will you be back in time for the rehearsal?'

'In lots of time,' Avril said. 'I'm only going to have lunch with Lynne.'

They went on chatting about the play, with Lucille returning, whenever she had the chance, to the impropriety of having cast Fred Dyer as Romeo. She was also against the part of Juliet having been given to Fred Dyer's girlfriend. I thought that perhaps she might be right there. The whole village knew of the relationship, and so were liable to take some of the more impassioned speeches as particularly titillating jokes. Some sniggering in the audience was only to be expected.

On our way home, Brian observed, 'I wonder if that girl, Sharon Whatshername, knows anything about her boyfriend's past. I didn't think this evening was the time to mention it, but I've a feeling she at least ought to know something about it.'

We had walked home with the Loxleys, leaving them and their three dogs at their gate. Peter had been very quiet all the evening. Not that he was ever very talkative, but it seemed to me that he had been more silent than usual. He gave the impression of having some serious worry on his mind, and I had my own private belief of what it might be, or at least to what it might be connected. Avril and Hugh's wife, Anna, had been close friends, and during Anna's long illness Avril had not only helped Hugh to nurse her, taking on herself as much of the burden of this as she could, but had slipped into a close and intimate relationship with Hugh. What Avril's feelings about him were I did not know, but I was fairly sure that if the rumour was right that he would remarry quite soon, I believed that if only she had not been married already, it would have been Avril whom he would have chosen.

Of course, if Avril did not respond, Peter would have no reason to worry, but it had seemed to me during the evening that her intimacy with Hugh had almost been put on display. His kiss of greeting to her on the Loxleys' arrival had been a great deal warmer than the light touch on the cheek that he had given me and he had held an arm around her for long enough to make her give a self-conscious little laugh, not really at all displeased, as she extricated herself from it. Hugh had talked to her quietly far more through the evening than to anyone else, while Peter, with a sullen look on his face, had talked mostly to Kevin, though this had meant taking on Lucille as well, while I had spent most of the time with Jane Kerwood and Brian, who had read her book and was charmed to meet her. Malcolm had wandered here and there, but had spent only a few minutes with Avril and Hugh, which had made me wonder if he had the same thoughts about their relationship as I had.

I had never discussed the matter with him, as I had had a feeling that he would have told me that village life was corrupting me into an old gossip and that I had better not start saying that sort of thing to anyone else. As I had no intention of doing so, or even of agreeing about it with anyone who might raise the subject with me, this would not have troubled me much, yet I had a feeling that sometime soon I should suddenly find myself telling Malcolm about my suspicions, mostly to find out if he did not share them. He was shrewd and observant and his years of work in a co-educational school had trained him in the noticing of when friendship was sliding into something that on occasion could be more dangerous.

But of course, in those days he had had to make up his mind whether or not he had a responsibility to interfere, something that he had intensely disliked doing and in fact had done only two or three times in all the years that we had been at Granborough, whereas now, whatever might be happening had nothing to do with him, even though he liked Peter and would not wish to see him hurt and humiliated. He liked Hugh too, and perhaps to a slightly lesser extent, Avril. I was not sure how much the dogs had to do with that. He had complained to me that it was almost impossible to have any contact with her undiluted by dogs which he found uninteresting.

Walking up the path to our door, Malcolm replied to Brian, 'So you believe in Dyer's guilt.'

'I didn't say that,' Brian said. 'I only said I thought that girl ought to know something about what this man was doing before he came here. Perhaps she does know and doesn't worry about his using a false name. I hope she does, because if not, there's something rather worrying about her playing Juliet to his Romeo.'

'I think you do believe in his guilt, all the same,' Malcolm said, as he opened our door and the three of us went into the sitting room.

'I'm not at all sure that I do,' Brian answered, as he dropped down on to the sofa. 'His leaving Edgewater suddenly and changing his name could have been the reaction of a sensitive man to the mere fact that he was suspected of three atrocious crimes and saw no way of absolutely clearing his name. And the little evidence they got was very thin. That he was red-haired. That a girl saw him and identified him and then changed her mind about it. That he'd bought some plastic bags. You could hardly accuse him on that, could you? And he'd a good reputation in the place. He hadn't been there long, only six months or so, but his employer was entirely satisfied with him, though he did say he was a bit of a queer 'un. A little too well-educated to be working in a garage, it seemed. He evidently tried not to show it, but didn't quite succeed. All the same . . .' He paused. 'Well, it's nothing to do with me. I'm not going to that girl of his with my story.'

'Do you suppose the Edgewater police know where he is?' Malcolm asked.

35

'I should think they certainly do,' Brian said.

'Have there been any other suspects?'

'Oh, several.'

'But no arrest.'

'Not yet.'

'Are they sure that it was an Edgewater man?'

'I don't think so. In these days of the car and the motor-bike, he might have come from anywhere. As all his murders seem to have happened in Edgewater, it would appear that the place has some meaning for him, even if he doesn't live there. Who knows, he might even have come from Raneswood. No . . .' Brian raised a hand to stop Malcolm interrupting him. 'That isn't entirely a joke. I've been wondering if anything special brought Benyon – or Dyer, if that's what you want to call him – if there was anything special that brought him here. Does he know something that the rest of us don't, and is he perhaps doing rather nicely out of it?'

For supper we had cold roast veal and salad, followed by biscuits and cheese, finishing up with coffee and brandy. Malcolm carved the veal while I made the salad. After-wards, we watched a play on television, then the news. We went to bed early. Malcolm and I were both in bed, with the light turned out, when, perhaps because I had had a little more to drink that evening than I was used to, I found myself saying the very thing to him that I had so far managed to keep to myself.

'Malcolm, has it ever struck you that Hugh's in love with Avril? Or if not exactly in love, say about halfway there? If she weren't married, don't you think she might quite soon replace Anna?'

'It's odd you should say that, because this evening I started wondering if Jane wasn't elected for that, though he's a bit old for her,' Malcolm replied. 'But did that never occur to you?'

'No, and I don't find the idea of it convincing,' I said.

36

'For one thing, if he were in love with Jane, why shouldn't he get on and do something about it? There's nothing to stop him is there?'

'Unless Jane herself has stopped him. Or perhaps he just doesn't like the idea of trekking across the Sahara on a camel, or perhaps next time it will be the Gobi desert, and he isn't sure he'll be able to keep her quietly in Raneswood, and is just plain scared.'

'Do you really think she'll be off on her travels again then?'

'Isn't it probable?'

'Perhaps. But you don't think I'm right that he cares about Avril?'

'I hadn't thought about it, but perhaps you are. But what d'you make of Avril's feelings? Is she going to divorce Peter, or stick to him?'

'I don't know if he's ever given her any grounds for divorce.'

'Can't that be done more or less by mutual agreement nowadays? I don't know quite how it works, but I know it's a lot easier than it was when we were young.'

'Suppose he wouldn't agree.'

'Which he probably wouldn't. I think he's a fairly possessive character.'

'Then they'd just have to follow the example of our Fred Dyer and Sharon, and live together, which reminds me, Malcolm . . .'

'Yes?'

'Oh, I was just going to ask you what you thought of Brian's belief that Fred is really someone called Jack Benyon, and that he's probably murdered three girls. But I'm not sure that I really want to talk about that at this time of night. It might give one nightmares.'

'I'm sure he's right that Fred's the man he used to see occasionally in Edgewater,' Malcolm said. 'It was so obvious when they saw each other that Fred recognized Brian. But Brian isn't sure about the murders, is he?'

'I think he is, you know, although he doesn't admit it.'

'Perhaps you're right. Well, sleep well.'

'Good night.'

'Good night.'

I fell asleep almost at once and did not dream of Fred, or murders, or divorces, but of crossing a wide open space on a bicycle which someone had informed me was usually called the Gobi desert, but that if I went on for long enough I would find out its real name, which was a very important thing to do and would win me a gold cup. However, I got lost in the desert and found myself cycling along Piccadilly to meet a famous film star, and I woke up before I found her.

Next morning, looking out of an upstairs window, I saw Avril leave for London in their BMW, and Mrs Henderson arrive punctually as usual at nine o'clock to do the Loxleys' cleaning. Soon after breakfast, Malcolm and Brian set off together for one of their long walks on the Downs. I began working on a chicken casserole for our lunch, then got out my shopping trolley and started off for the village, where there was a store that stocked nearly everything and made frequent trips into Otterswell unnecessary.

Raneswood is one of those long, straggling villages with only a few byroads leading off the main road that runs through it. Our village hall was at one of the bends in the road, with ample parking space round it. It was a fairly new acquisition in the village and we were all rather proud of it. It had a hall big enough for a badminton court, with a stage at one end of it, so that it could easily be converted into a theatre, and a small lending library, cared for on a voluntary basis by two or three old people who lived in a retirement home nearby and had nothing else to do. There was also a small kitchen so that it was easy to serve coffee or even more ambitious refreshments when one of the village societies held a meeting there. It was there, of course, that the dramatic society was due to meet that evening for our first rehearsal.

I passed it and went on to the store, where I filled my trolley with fruit and vegetables, cheese, tea, and various kinds of tinned food, besides two bottles of Tio Pepe, which was about all that it would hold, and I was just leaving when I met Jane Kerwood coming in. It was at her suggestion that as soon as she had done her shopping, which she said would take only a minute, we should cross the road to the Green Man and have coffee together. The Green Man was a comfortable old pub which had recently taken to serving coffee as well as alcoholic drinks, and where it was possible to have a reasonably good lunch, or to pick up a takeaway meal. Jane did her shopping, then the two of us crossed the road, went into the pub, found a pleasant corner in the bar, which was almost empty at that time, then ordered our coffee and settled down for a chat.

I asked her if she was thinking of some more travelling and writing another book.

She answered, 'I might write the book, but I haven't any more travelling in view. For one thing, I don't think I could afford it. It comes quite expensive.'

'What would the book be about then?' I asked.

'About all the things I didn't write about in the last one,' she said. 'But I don't suppose I shall really do it.'

'What made you do it last time?'

She hesitated, then with a curious change of expression on her friendly, gentle face, almost as if she had suddenly decided to be a different person for the moment, she said, 'I thought it might cure a broken heart.'

I did not believe she was serious, because she was smiling, so I felt it safe to ask, 'And did it work?'

'I'm not sure,' she said. 'What I really think it taught me was that I hadn't a heart to break. To think of some of the things that I've seen, and then think of how comfortably I live in Raneswood, suggests that this thing

39

throbbing away inside me is just a muscular pump.'

'If you could get under the surface, even here in Raneswood,' I said, 'you might find that a lot of the muscular pumps give their owners plenty of pain.'

Her soft brown eyes studied me thoughtfully and after a moment she said, 'Have you anyone special in mind?'

'Oh no,' I said. 'I'm just generalizing about the human condition.'

As if she knew that I was not being entirely truthful, she gave a little shake of her head.

'I could name several, I think, but perhaps it would be wiser not to,' she said. 'It's one of the reasons I can't make up my mind to start another book. I enjoyed writing the last one, and it added very pleasantly to my income, but if I wrote another, I think I'd find myself going into things quite differently from last time, going under the surface of all sorts of things I only wrote about as an almost casual observer. And I don't think I've got the courage to do that. My real reason for setting out on that journey, for instance. When I started, I hadn't any intention of writing about it. I just very badly wanted to get away. The book was a sort of bonus that I hadn't expected.'

'So you meant what you said about trying to cure a broken heart?'

It might have been a cruel thing to say, only I had a feeling that she wanted to talk about it. However, I seemed to be wrong, for she laughed and said, 'Oh, don't take me so seriously. I'm one of the people who was born with a broken heart. You've probably never seen me in one of my bad moods, but it was in one of them that I set out on my travels. I'd just emerged from what seemed a never-ending depression and I was terrified of slipping into another, so off I went to take a look at people who were more miserable than I was. I expect that sounds very cold-blooded, but on the whole it worked.'

I did not really believe that she was telling me the truth. I felt that she was in a mood of wanting to confide something far more personal, but that the lack of courage of which she had spoken made her draw back every time she came near to doing so. There was no reason, however, why I should press her to do more than she wanted.

To change the subject, I asked, 'By the way, what do you think of our Romeo? He's a strange young man and I've started wondering if we made a mistake in choosing him.'

'I hardly know him,' she answered. 'I do rather wonder how we'll feel about hearing Shakespeare spoken in that accent of his.'

'That accent can miraculously disappear when he's in the mood for it,' I said. 'Anyway, we'll hear how it goes this evening. If it's too bad we might be able to get him to give up the part, and find someone else to do it.'

'And whom do you suggest should take it over? Not Kevin!'

'I doubt if Kevin would want to do it.'

'Oh, he'd do it if Lucille got to work on him, so if you want him, get to work on Lucille.'

'D'you think he'd really be suitable with that little pug-dog face of his?'

'Is there any reason why people with pug-dog faces shouldn't fall passionately in love?'

I wanted to tell her the story that Brian had told us about Fred Dyer's past and see if she felt that someone with such a shadow hanging over them should be our Romeo, but a certain doubt of the story that I felt made me change the subject again. Presently, we finished our coffee and parted at the door of the Green Man, going in opposite directions to our homes, each of us trailing her shopping trolley behind her.

It was nearly twelve o'clock when we set off, and by the time that I reached our gate, it was exactly twelve, and there, as I approached it, punctual to the minute as she always was, both in arriving and leaving, I saw Mrs

Henderson emerging from the Loxleys' door and starting down the path to their gate.

I also saw something else that somewhat surprised me. Fred Dyer was standing at their gate, looking as if he was intending to go in, but was for some reason hesitating to do so. This was surprising for several reasons. One was that when he came to work in the Loxleys' garden or in ours, he always arrived in the van that contained his tools, but now there was no sign of it. He must have walked up from the flat in the old vicarage where he lived with Sharon. Another thing was that twelve o'clock was an unusual time for him to come. It was too late for a morning's work and too early for an afternoon's. It made me wonder for a moment if actually he was just leaving, but I saw him put a hand on the latch of the gate and push it open. Also, it was obvious that he had heard me coming, for he looked round at me, but then, instead of his usual smile and somewhat aloof greeting, he turned away quickly as if he did not want to have to speak to me. I said, 'Good morning, Fred,' and he grunted something in reply, but did not look round at me again.

Starting up the path to the house, he came face to face with Mrs Henderson. So far as I knew, he and she were on good terms, but today he simply strode past her and went straight to the side door of the house which I knew was rarely locked and let himself in. A wild barking of dogs greeted him. It reminded me that Avril was not there that morning. She had gone to London to have lunch with her famous cousin. The dogs were in Peter's charge and were always more restless and nervous than when Avril was there.

Mrs Henderson saw me and hurried along the path as if she wanted to speak to me, so I waited before going in at our gate.

'Well! Did you see that?' she asked as she came up to me.

'See what?' I asked.

'He cut me dead,' she said. 'Didn't even look at me, didn't answer when I said "Hello!" And what's he doing here at this time of day? He isn't even expected today; I know that because I spoke to Mr Loxley. I said, "This kitchen tap is dripping worse, you did ought to get it seen to." And he said, "We'll see if Fred can fix it for us one day," but he didn't say anything about today, as he would have done, wouldn't he, if he thought he could get hold of him today?'

'Perhaps he did manage to get hold of him,' I said. 'Miss Sawyer's got a telephone. He might have rung up and been lucky and got Fred.'

'And you think Fred's fed up at being dragged out when he usually takes Saturdays off, and that's why he wouldn't even say, "Hello!" to me? It don't seem likely somehow. He's in a bad temper or something all right, but why should he be rude to me? He's a queer young fellow, that's my opinion. I'm not sure if I'd have him around the place if it was for me to decide. And this living with a girlfriend – well, I know it's all the thing nowadays, but it doesn't feel right to me. If Miss Sawyer was my daughter, I wouldn't be too happy about it. Not that I'm criticizing anybody. Live and let live. But he didn't ought to have cut me dead like that, now did he?'

'I shouldn't worry too much about it,' I said. Yet I had a feeling, like Mrs Henderson, that there had been something oddly wrong, something out of character about Fred's behaviour. 'Something's probably upset him. He may have gone in to see Mr Loxley to see if he could give him some advice about some trouble that's come up, or something like that.'

The dogs were still barking as hard as ever. They did not seem to have welcomed Fred in a particularly friendly fashion.

'That's right,' Mrs Henderson said. 'Yes, I'm sure you're right, Mrs Chance. He's upset. But still, I don't really see why he should be rude to me. Young people nowadays, I don't understand them. Well, goodbye then.'

'Goodbye.'

She set off down the lane to the village, and I went up the path to our door.

Malcolm and Brian had not yet got back from their walk. The house was empty. I went into the kitchen and unpacked my trolley, then I started preparing some vegetables to go with the chicken casserole that I had left in the oven, and making a fresh fruit salad. It was while I was doing that that a strange thing happened.

I heard a shot.

What now seems to me the strangest thing about it was that at the time I took almost no notice of it. Someone, I thought, was shooting at rabbits that had got into his vegetable garden. They had a way of getting into some of our gardens from the woods behind us, and one or two of our neighbours, I knew, had a way of trying to scare them away by shooting. In a moment, I had forgotten about it. Malcolm and Brian came in and we settled down to drinking sherry before I dished up the chicken casserole. They had had a very good walk and Brian could hardly find words to describe the beauties of the Downs on a spring morning of the kind that we were having. The sky was a pale, fresh blue, the sunshine glittering. He exclaimed at the distance that they had been able to see across the gently rolling green hills and said that I ought to have been with them.

I replied that I could go on the walk that they had taken any day of the week, and that I was sure that they were happy to be able to walk at their own pace, instead of having to slow down for me, and talk as much shop as they liked. I told them that I had had coffee with Jane Kerwood, but did not choose to tell them all the things that we had talked about, though I had a feeling that something had happened that might have interested

44

them, though for some reason I could not think what it was.

We had more sherry, then our lunch, then Brian said he felt like a sleep and went to lie down in his room and Malcolm went to his study to try to do a little work on his autobiography.

I suspected that he actually fell asleep as soundly as Brian, for I heard no sound from his typewriter, and I fell asleep myself for a while in a chair in the sitting room, then, when I woke, picked up my copy of *Romeo and Juliet* and started studying my part. I had had a good memory when I was young and could have learnt my lines in no time, but it was going to take some hard work, I recognized, to do it now. About half-past four, I made some tea and called the two men down to it.

It was at about five o'clock, when we were still sitting round the tea-table, that the doorbell rang.

Whoever was ringing kept their finger on the bell for so long that it had a sound of excitement about it, of impatience and perhaps of distress. Then, before Malcolm could reach the door, the ringing stopped and our door-knocker was violently pounded. He opened the door and Avril took a swift step inside, then almost fell into his arms. If he had not caught her it looked as if she would have fallen. Her face was dead white and her eyes were wide and staring.

'Oh, Malcolm, help me!' she gasped. 'I can't go in there again all by myself. It's too awful!'

He led her forward into the sitting room.

'What is it, Avril?' he asked.

'He's dead, he's stone dead!' she cried. 'Peter – lying on the floor in the hall. There's a gun beside him – his gun – and there's blood all over his face. And half of his face isn't there. Oh, please help me. Tell me what I ought to do!'

CHAPTER 3

Malcolm took charge. He could always be relied on to take charge in a time of serious crisis, just as certainly as he would avoid having anything to do with the minor crises that occur continuously in domestic life. When the boys' wing at Granborough had gone on fire one night, due to some child's practical joke that had gone wrong, he had taken control with grave-faced equanimity, got all the boys out into the quad, directed the school fire brigade until the fire brigade from Edgewater arrived, and had given no sign of the anxiety that he was feeling internally. But if his pyjamas did not come back from the laundry, or if we ran out of sherry, it was for me to put the matter right. What we had on our hands at the moment was a very serious crisis, and as a matter of course, he took charge.

'I'll go over and Brian will come with me,' he said. 'You stay here with Frances, Avril. Can we get into the house? Is the door unlocked?'

He had handed Avril on to me by then. I had her in my arms and felt her violent shuddering. She clung to me for a moment, then jerked herself away.

'Yes, it's unlocked, but I've got to go over with you,' she said. 'I must.'

'No, no, you must stay here,' Malcolm said. 'If a doctor's needed, we'll phone for Redfield, and if it looks as if we've got to get the police. We'll phone the people in Otterswell. But there's no need to inflict all that on you.'

'Of course it's the police you'll need,' Avril said, her

voice unnaturally shrill. Her face was colourless, but her eyes looked unusually large and luminous, with a shine that might have come from fear. 'But I've got to go back with you. The dogs are shut up in the kitchen and they're going crazy. They know something terrible's happened, though they can't know what, and they're making a fearful noise and trying to break the door down. I don't know why they're shut up in the kitchen. Peter wouldn't have put them there like that. I suppose the – the murderer did it, but I don't know how he managed it. They never obey anyone but Peter and me.'

'The bloody dogs!' Malcolm said. 'Sorry, Avril, but it doesn't sound as if they're the most important thing at the moment. But come with us if you must.' He looked at me. 'Coming, Frances?'

'Yes,' I said.

'I shouldn't have come rushing round like this,' Avril said, trying to sound calmer, 'but I couldn't stand it in there alone. And I'd a feeling he – the man – whoever it was – might still be there, though I knew he wasn't. Peter's stone cold. I think he's been dead for hours. And the man wouldn't have stayed around all that time, would he? If he went in to steal, he'd have had plenty of time to find there was nothing much worth taking. A little jewellery, a little money in Peter's wallet. He could have found those at once and got away hours ago. All the same, I was frightened.'

'Well, let's go, shall we?' Malcolm said. He put an arm round her shoulders. 'Of course you were frightened. Who wouldn't be? And coming here was the obvious thing to do. I only hope we can help a bit in some way.'

He drew her back to the door. I hesitated. There were several things I wanted to say, but I was fairly sure this was not the time to say them. I looked at Brian and he gave a little shake of his head, almost as if he were telling me that now was not the time to talk, though really I think he was telling me to leave Avril to Malcolm. We went out of the house behind them, down the path to the gate and along the lane to the Loxleys' gate, and up the path to their door. It was wide open and the noise that the dogs were making reached us while we were still in the lane.

A heap of something that I was afraid to look at was at the foot of the stairs. I had seen dead people before in my life, but they had all been calmly and decently laid out in bed, with their eyes closed and the set of their features serenely peaceful. They had not had one side of their head half blasted away, and their one remaining eye staring fiercely into nothingness. Peter looked as if he had been very angry at being killed. There was a good deal of blood on what was left of his face and on his shirt, and near him on the floor lay a revolver, with one of his hands looking as if it were reaching for it. But I did not think for a moment that it was he who had fired it, or if he had, it had not been at himself.

Avril had gone straight into the kitchen and had shut the door behind her. The barking of the dogs stopped at once. Malcolm stooped over the dead man on the floor and felt one of his hands.

'Yes, stone cold,' he said, 'and rigor beginning. This happened a good while ago.'

'I think I know when it happened,' I said. 'A little after twelve o'clock. I think I heard a shot.'

He turned his head quickly to look at me.

'D'you mean that?'

'Yes.'

'You'll have to tell the police about it.'

'Of course.'

'Well, I'll phone them now.' He looked round, saw that there was no telephone in the hall, then said, 'What's happened to Avril?'

'And the dogs,' I said.

'She's taken them out into the garden, I should think,' Brian said. 'Sensible thing to do.'

'Anyway, where's the telephone?' Malcolm asked me, as if noticing such things was more the kind of thing that I should do than could be expected of him.

He happened to be right, for not only had I been in the house far more often than him, drinking coffee and gossiping with Avril, but I do notice such things and he does not. He could have been in their drawing room, where as a matter of fact the telephone was, a dozen times and afterwards not be able to tell you what colour the curtains were, or what pictures were on their walls.

I led the way into the drawing room, a high, elegant room with tall sash windows overlooking a garden that was fading into the twilight. Brian was right about Avril. She was on the sweep of lawn that stretched from the house to a high old wall of rosy brick, half-hidden in creepers. She was throwing a ball for the dogs to chase. I was not sure if it shocked me or if I admired her. It was a way of keeping them employed and out of the way in a manner that I should certainly have admired if they had been young children whom it was important to save from understanding the horror that was in the house. But they were not young children, they were dogs, and what she was doing simply left all responsibility for what had to be done now to us.

'Do you think we ought to get her inside, so that she knows what you say to the police?' Brian said.

'It looks as if she'd rather leave it to us to get on with it.' Malcolm's tone was sardonic. 'And the sooner we do it, the better.'

He made the call to the police in Otterswell, and after a little explaining was put through to someone whose name apparently was Detective Inspector Holroyd, who told him to stay where he was, touch nothing, and wait for the arrival of the police, which would be as prompt as possible. Malcolm put the telephone down and gave a deep sigh.

'Didn't you say you came to Raneswood for peace and quiet?' he said to Brian.

'It's usually one of its attractions,' Brian answered.

Malcolm threw himself down on a sofa. I had sat down in one of the deep armchairs near the fireplace and Brian had gone to one of the windows and was gazing out, as if the sight of Avril throwing the ball and the dogs happily chasing it had a sort of fascination for him.

'About the shot you heard,' Malcolm said to me, 'how did that happen?'

'I'd been down to the village,' I said, 'to do some shopping, and I met Jane there and we had a coffee together in the Green Man. Then I came home and the reason I know it was just about twelve o'clock when I got here is that Mrs Henderson was coming out of their house, and you know how punctual she is. She arrives on the dot of nine and leaves exactly at twelve. But as it happened, Fred Dyer was arriving just then, and he went up to the house and in at the side door, which was a bit odd for several reasons.'

Brian turned quickly when he heard the name.

'Fred Dyer? He was here?'

'Yes. But as I said, it was a bit odd. I wouldn't say that he's normally the most friendly of human beings, but when we meet he generally greets me and says a thing or two about the weather, but this morning he did neither. He literally turned his back on me, so that as I remember it, I didn't even see his face. And it was the same when he met Mrs Henderson halfway up the path. He looked away, as if he didn't want to see her . . .'

'Just a minute,' Malcolm interrupted. 'You're sure of all this, are you?'

'Oh, yes.'

'Because you'll have to tell it all to the police.'

'Of course.'

'And wasn't it a bit peculiar, his coming here at twelve o'clock? He usually works for the Loxleys in the afternoon.'

'That's one of the things I was going to say,' I said. 'But

he might have dropped in to change some arrangement he'd made with them, or something like that. The other thing that I thought was really odd was that he'd come on foot, not in his van. He always comes in his van when he comes up here, but this morning he walked.'

'Suppose that girlfriend of his had wanted the van for some reason.'

'She's got her own car.'

'Hm. Yes. It is a bit strange. But what happened next? I mean, about the shot you heard.'

'Well, I went home and started on a bit of cooking, and suddenly I heard what sounded like a shot. It would have been about a quarter of an hour after I got in.'

'And naturally you took no notice of it.'

'No, I thought it was someone shooting at rooks or rabbits, or it could even have been a back-fire on the road. I didn't give it a thought until – well, until Avril came in this evening.'

'And you could have been right about the rooks and rabbits. It may not have been the shot that killed Peter that you heard.'

'I see one's got to take that into consideration,' I said, 'but it would have been a bit of a coincidence if it wasn't.'

'Fred Dyer,' Brian said. 'Jack Benyon. If he shot Loxley, then he's changed his *modus operandi*. No plastic bag and strangling this time. Unusual in murderers, I believe, but I suppose not unheard of. I wonder what he had against Loxley?'

'Now let's not jump to conclusions,' Malcolm said. 'That's strictly for the police. Ah, Avril . . .' For she had just appeared at the drawing room door. 'I've phoned the police. They'll be here as soon as possible.'

'I've shut the dogs up in the kitchen again,' she said, as if that was the most important thing she had to tell us. 'And I've given them their supper. They'll be quiet now that they know I'm back.'

'Frances, don't you think you should tell Avril what you've just been telling us?' Malcolm said.

I could see myself having to tell the story a number of times before the evening was out. I would have to tell it to Detective Inspector Holroyd, and perhaps to some other policemen, and now there was no question that I would have to tell it to Avril. But she seemed hardly interested. Her haggard face was blank and empty. She was in a state of shock, I thought, and it might be a good idea to look for some brandy. I remembered having been told that the right treatment for shock was hot, very sweet tea, but to make tea I should have to go into the kitchen and deal with the three dogs, probably upsetting them and starting them barking again. I should also have had to go towards the hall, passing close to that tragic thing that lay on the floor at the foot of the stairs. I asked Avril whether there was any brandy in the house.

She pointed at a fine old cabinet between the windows, and dropped into a chair. Brian went to the cabinet and took out brandy and four glasses. He filled them and brought them to Malcolm and me, keeping one for himself when he had given one to Avril.

'What is it Frances ought to tell me?' she asked. Her voice had lost its shrillness and was merely flat and dead.

I told her the story that I had told the others.

'Fred Dyer,' she muttered, as if it was not a matter of much importance. 'I don't know what he was doing here. He wasn't coming here to work today.'

'You weren't expecting him for any reason?' Malcolm asked.

She shook her head wearily. It was then that I noticed that tears were trickling out of her eyes and down her cheeks. She sipped her brandy.

'Perhaps Peter had thought of some job he wanted him to do,' she said. 'Our shower keeps going wrong. It's the hard water. It gets choked up. He might have rung Fred up and asked him to come and see to it.'

'Hardly a reason for murder,' Brian said.

'And wouldn't Dyer have come in his van with his tools, instead of on foot?' Malcolm said.

'I don't know. Perhaps he would.' Her thoughts seemed to be a long way off.

'What were the relations between your husband and Dyer?' Brian asked.

'Relations?' she said. 'There weren't any that I know of. I mean, when Fred came here to work in the garden or do odd jobs for us, it was always I who coped with him. I told him what we wanted done and paid him.'

'Did he know that you were going to London today?' Brian went on.

'I don't know. Perhaps. Yes. I think he did. I think I told him when he was working here yesterday that I was going to London to meet my cousin, Lynne Denison. I've been telling everybody. I'm such a fool. And he knew who she was, and he was thrilled about it. He asked if she'd be coming here and if she did, would he have a chance to see her. I told him I didn't know.'

'You're thinking he knew Peter would be here alone,' Malcolm said to Brian.

'Well, that might be important, mightn't it?' Brian answered.

'But why should he come when he was almost certain to run into Mrs Henderson?' Malcolm asked. 'He must have known the ways of the house, that she'd be leaving at twelve. He'd only to wait ten minutes and she wouldn't have seen him. As it is, she'll be able to corroborate Frances's story.'

'Be quiet, be quiet!' Avril suddenly shouted at him. 'Can't you see you're driving me mad?' And gulping down her brandy, she broke into violent sobbing. Her whole body shook as her voice went up almost into a shriek.

The two men looked a little ashamed of themselves, as if they had only just recognized what a strain she was under. As if the dogs could hear her and were scared and angry at what was happening, they began to bark. I put my arms round Avril and she clung to me like a child.

'We'd better stop this,' Malcolm muttered. 'It's not our job to try to work things out.'

With her head against my breast, Avril spoke in a voice thick with her sobs. 'Fred didn't do it. Why should he?'

'Yes, why?' Brian said. 'And why is he here in Raneswood? And where did that gun come from?'

'Let's leave all that to the police,' Malcolm said, drinking up his brandy. 'They won't thank us for interfering.'

This turned out to be true. When the police arrived, they seemed only to want us to get out of the way. As Detective Inspector Holroyd, to whom Malcolm had spoken on the telephone, asked where we had come from and how it happened that we were there on the spot, and when we told him that we lived next door and that Mrs Loxley had come to us for help, he asked us to return to our home and wait for him there. He would be over soon and would have a great many questions to ask us, but for the present he would like a chance to view the scene of the crime without our company.

He was a tall, burly man with a square, heavy face in which a pair of small, very bright brown eyes were sunk deep under brows that tilted at their ends in a way that gave him an oddly pixie-like look. Indeed, if he could have been shrunk down to a foot or so, instead of being the six foot two that he certainly was, he would not have been unlike a garden gnome. Although he could not have been much over forty, his thick hair was almost white, merely streaked with tufts of grey. He was courteous and calm, taking murder, or, as he pointed out, perhaps suicide or misadventure – it was too early to come to any conclusion – as something about which he was not inclined to make too much of a fuss.

'And perhaps you'd better take the dogs with you,' he said to Avril, once he had discovered to whom they belonged. 'Natural they shouldn't care for all of us tramping around.'

By then there were a number of men in the house, and several cars in the lane.

Avril, who had grown oddly calm with their coming, collected the dogs and the four of us left the house and went along the lane and in at our gate.

It was dark by then. When we entered the house, the first thing that had to be done was to deal with the dogs. Avril had put them all on leads, and though the unfamiliar men and cars as we walked along the lane had made them nervous, they seemed tired and ready to settle down anywhere that was sufficiently comfortable. The retriever stretched himself out on our sofa, the Labrador in an easy-chair and the Belgian shepherd on the hearthrug. Avril seemed inclined to make the ones that had annexed our chairs get out of them, but Malcolm told her not to bother, and to leave them in peace. In a few minutes, the retriever was snoring.

It was Avril who suddenly said, 'The rehearsal!'

'Yes,' Malcolm said, 'we'll have to put it off. We'll have to phone round and tell people not to come.' He looked at me. 'Could you do that?'

'I suppose so,' I said, 'but what do we tell them? I don't feel like breaking the news a dozen times or so that we've had a murder.'

'Say that Peter's been taken ill and it's no use our trying to go ahead without Mercutio.'

'Anyway, the news will be all round the place almost at once,' Brian said. 'All those police cars in the lane won't have gone unnoticed.'

'I imagine we're going to cancel the whole thing,' I said. 'I can't see our going ahead with it in the circumstances.'

'Oh, you mustn't do that!' Avril cried. 'Peter wouldn't have wanted it. But of course, I'll step out of it and you can get someone else to take my part. Jane Kerwood, for instance.'

'No, I think everyone will want to call it off,' Malcolm said. 'It would be difficult to put on a cheerful sort of show when one of the cast has only recently been killed.'

'But *Romeo and Juliet* isn't a cheerful sort of show,' Avril protested. 'It's very tragic.'

'Of course, of course, but in our hands, at the best of times, the tragedy might not have been too successful. And we don't want to find ourselves playing to an audience that's come mostly out of morbid curiosity.'

'But Lynne said she'd come,' Avril said. 'I told her all about it, and she was quite interested, and she promised to come down sometime soon to see if she could help us. And I'm sure she meant it. And everyone will be so disappointed if we put her off.'

'She can come if she wants to, even if we aren't going ahead with our play.' Malcolm turned to me. 'What about that telephoning?'

'Yes,' I said, 'but I'm just thinking that we must arrange what Avril's going to do tonight. She can't go back to that house. You'll stay here with us, won't you, Avril?'

'That's very good of you,' she said. 'It's true that nothing would make me spend the night over there, but I could go to the Green Man. I don't want to put you out.'

'It won't be putting us out at all,' I said. 'That's settled, you're staying here. One of us can go over later and fetch the things you'll need, if you'll tell us where they are, or you can borrow from me if those men are still there and don't want to let anyone in to take anything away.'

'Have we got the numbers of all the people you'll have to phone?' Malcolm asked.

'I think so,' I said. 'I've got the numbers of everyone in the society.'

'Then let's get ahead with the job.'

Our telephone was on a table in the hall, with a chair beside it, and a book on the table that contained all the numbers that we most frequently used. I had just sat down in the chair and opened the book when the telephone rang.

I picked it up and said, 'Frances Chance speaking.'

'This is Hugh,' he said, which was unnecessary, as I knew his voice. 'Frances, what's happened? All those police cars at the Loxleys' house and the ambulance and all the men! Has there been an accident or something?'

'It looks as if it's something worse than an accident,' I said. I thought that his call was only the first that we should be having. The other people who lived along the lane must have seen what he had, and I saw no point in telling him anything but the truth. 'Peter's dead,' I said. 'He's been shot and it's almost certainly murder. Incidentally, I was just going to ring you up to tell you that we've decided the rehearsal will have to be cancelled.'

'Of course it will. Dead? Murdered? Do you mean it? Frances, how terrible. Have they any idea who could have done such a thing?'

'It's too early to say,' I said.

'Can I help in any way? Is there anything I can do? I suppose you were going to phone round all the people who should have been at the rehearsal. Can I do that for you?'

'Oh, would you do that, Hugh? I'd be so grateful.'

'Telling them about the murder?'

'We were going to say that Peter's been taken ill, but if you feel like telling them the truth, I don't see anything against it.'

In fact, I thought it the best thing to do, as long as it was not I who had to do it.

'Only I don't know anything about it,' Hugh said. 'What actually happened?'

'You could say it looks as if someone broke into the house and killed Peter when he caught him. That's as much as anyone knows at the moment.'

'All right, I'll go ahead with it. And if there's anything else I can do, let me know. How's Avril?'

'In a state of shock, I think. She seems confused about what is and what isn't important. But we're looking after her. She's going to spend the night here.'

'Good, good.'

He rang off. I put the telephone down and returned to the sitting room.

'That was Hugh,' I said. 'He's going to do the phoning for us.'

'And now what about a bit of supper?' Malcolm said. 'There's no point in waiting for the police. They may not come round for hours.'

In fact, they came about half an hour later. Detective Inspector Holroyd, I thought, looked even more like an outsize garden gnome than I remembered, and he had a sergeant with him, a slim, trim-looking, wide-shouldered young man, with a fresh pink face which he took care to keep expressionless. They interviewed us one by one in the dining room, beginning with Avril and ending with me. The sergeant took copious notes in a notebook. By the time that my turn came, the notebook looked pretty well filled. They were both sitting at the table and the inspector gestured to me to take a seat facing them.

'Your husband told us you have something of interest to tell us,' he said.

'Didn't he tell you himself what it was?' I asked.

'He told us one or two things, but I'd be grateful if you would tell us about it yourself. Something about hearing a shot, and seeing a man at the Loxleys' gate. Can you describe him to us?'

'I can do more than that,' I said. 'I can tell you who he was.'

'Ah, that's something your husband didn't tell us. He said he preferred to leave it to you to tell us. Quite correct, too. Can you name him then?'

'He's called Fred Dyer, and he lives with a girl called

59

Sharon Sawyer in a flat in the old vicarage. He turned up in Raneswood a few months ago and seems to make a living of a sort doing odd jobs about the village.'

'And you saw him at the Loxleys' gate as you came home from shopping?'

'Yes, and I think the time was just about twelve o'clock, because Mrs Henderson, who does the cleaning for the Loxleys, was just coming out of the house, and she always leaves the house exactly at twelve o'clock. She'll corroborate what I can tell you.'

'And you're sure this man you saw was Fred Dyer?'

'Oh, yes.'

'You couldn't possibly be mistaken about that?'

'No, why should I be?'

'You know him quite well?'

'Yes, he's worked for us from time to time.'

'Did you speak to him?'

'Only to say hello in passing.'

'But there's no possibility you could be mistaken about who it was?'

'Well, as a matter of fact . . .' I hesitated. 'No, it's just a sort of an idea I had, it doesn't mean anything.' But something had been worrying me and I was half inclined to tell him about it, though I felt it would only sound ridiculous. 'It's just that there was something unusual about the way he behaved, but I suppose that was only to be expected if he was intending to commit a murder.'

'Yes?' he prompted me.

'Well, he didn't look at me, but sort of turned away as I came by, and he did the same with Mrs Henderson,' I said. 'And he'd come on foot instead of in the van he usually uses.'

'But you're sure all the same it was Benyon – I mean – Dyer, whom you saw?'

I felt that he had deliberately made the mistake to see how I would react to it.

'Oh, Mr Hewlett's been telling you that he thinks Dyer

60

is a man he knew in Edgewater called Benyon,' I said, without sounding too interested. 'I don't know anything about that, except that when Dyer saw Mr Hewlett when we were bringing him home from the station, he looked very startled, as if he recognized him. But that could have been a mistake.'

'Quite so, except that we've been keeping an eye on Dyer since he came here. The Edgewater people tipped us off. They knew where he went when he left Edgewater. In fact, I think he told them himself where he was going. He told them he couldn't stand the atmosphere of suspicion that had developed around him in Edgewater, and that he was going to change his name. But you understand why I'm anxious to know if your identification of him as the man at the gate is absolutely positive, because it looks as if he was the victim of one false identification a little while ago. Not that we're absolutely certain it was false. He may have been the Edgewater murderer, though I've believed all along that he was innocent. He's a too normal sort of man to go in for the kind of murders that happened there.'

'But not too normal to do some straightforward shooting?' I said.

'It would be a curious change in MO, if he was guilty of both kinds of killing,' he said. 'However, it isn't impossible that he was. To return to what we were saying, you're absolutely certain it was Dyer you saw at the gate?'

Each time he asked me that, I felt less certain. The uneasiness that I had felt from the start about that meeting had developed into a definite doubt.

'I suppose I just could be mistaken,' I said uncertainly. 'He did keep his face turned away. But he's a distinctive looking man. That red hair of his and his build – he's tall and very well-made – it wouldn't be easy for anyone to disguise himself as Dyer.'

'But not impossible?'

61

'All right, I'll say it's not impossible, but I don't believe it.'

'And I'm sure you're right. This is just a matter of routine, you know. Tomorrow we'd like to have you sign a statement about it. Now, about the shot you heard, as your husband told us.'

So I told him how I had heard a shot, but had taken no notice of it, and after that he thanked me for being so cooperative and let me go. A few minutes after that, he and the sergeant left, and I went out to the kitchen to put together the supper which I had begun on when the two men arrived. We had cold chicken and salad and biscuits and cheese. No one was hungry and no one was much inclined to talk. But as we were finishing, Malcolm said, 'About the things that Avril will need, if she'll make a list of them I'll go over and do my best to find them.'

'I think it would be better if I went,' I said. 'I'm more likely to be able to find them. But a list would be useful.'

Avril made a list of the few things that she would need for the night, with some notes of where she kept them, and I was about to set out to collect them, when Brian said, 'I'll come with you.'

'It's all right, I don't mind going alone,' I said. 'The lane's still crawling with policemen. I imagine you could hardly find a safer place.'

'All the same, I'll come,' he said. 'You may have to argue your way into the house and I might be useful.'

So we set out together, Brian carrying a small suitcase while I had Avril's list of what she wanted. She had not even dropped a suggestion that she might get them herself and none of us expected her to do so, but as Brian and I started down the path to the gate, I found myself wondering how long she would actually be staying with us. What we were to collect that evening would be sufficient for one night, but next day, assuming that she would not dream of going back to live in her home, a new supply would be needed. And afterwards, what would she do?

62

She was welcome to stay with us for the present, but she was unlikely to want to do it for long, and where else would she think of going?

It might be necessary for her to remain in Raneswood, at least until after the inquest, but it seemed to me unlikely that she would want to stay on, now that she was alone and with a house on her hands in which she could not face the thought of living. I thought that she might move to London, except for the problem of the dogs. She and Peter had their small flat there, and that could be a refuge at least for a time, until she had got over the worst of the shock of Peter's death and was able to think lucidly about what she wanted to do with her life.

If she did not think of doing that herself, I thought, I would suggest it to her. Not immediately, of course. I was ready to be a good neighbour for a while. But I was a little afraid that she might find Malcolm and me comfortable sort of people to cling to in her troubles. She and her dogs. I did not much like the idea of giving her dogs a home. How different it would have been if there had been children, I thought. The children that according to Lucille she ought to have had. Of course, it was not too late for her to do something about it now. If she were to remarry and if no children came, might not another husband be ready to adopt a child? There had been a time when Malcolm and I had considered adoption, but he had always had more than enough children to cope with in his work, and I, though I always liked them once they were five or six years old and able to converse rationally, had never had really strong maternal feelings.

We were at the gate when Brian said, 'That policeman knew all about Fred Dyer.'

'Yes, so he told me,' I answered. 'But he wanted me to say I wasn't sure that it was Fred I saw at the Loxleys' gate, and he put such pressure on me to say it that I almost did.'

'But you didn't?' Brian said.

'I'm not sure. I believe I admitted it was possible I was wrong, or something near it.'

'And what do you think now?'

'Oh, I'm sure it was Fred. That's to say . . .'

'Well?' he said, as I paused.

'I suppose it just could have been someone dressed up as Fred. I mean, someone in a red wig, and of course his black leather jacket and jeans. You see, there were several rather peculiar things about the situation if it really was Fred. One is that he may have known that Avril was going to be in London, and gone into the house to steal what he could, but he'd have known that Peter would be there. The place wouldn't have been empty.'

'The motive wasn't robbery,' Brian said. 'The inspector told me that there were a hundred and twenty pounds in Peter's wallet, and Avril's jewellery hadn't been touched. No, someone went to that house with the single intention of killing Peter, and when she's more herself Avril may be able to tell us more about that – if she will.'

'What do you mean?' I asked.

'Only that it could have been convenient for her to be in London when it happened and that she knows more about it than she's likely to tell us.'

'Brian, what a perfectly horrible idea!'

'I'm not very serious about it,' he said as we reached the Loxleys' gate, 'only in any case of murder I believe the first person to be suspected is always the husband or wife. And you must admit it's convenient for her to have such an unbreakable alibi.'

'Perhaps Fred has an alibi too.'

'So you aren't too sure the man you saw was him.'

'I don't know, I don't know!' I was bewildered and a little angry. 'Let's not talk about it. It only confuses me. Let's get Avril's things and go home.'

But getting Avril's things was not so very easy. There were a number of men in the house, but Detective Inspector Holroyd was not there, nor was the young sergeant who had accompanied him when he came over to us, and we had to convince a sceptical uniformed sergeant that we were the neighbours with whom Mrs Loxley was staying and that we had only come to collect a few things for her.

In the end, he let us in, but when we went upstairs to the bedroom that she had shared with Peter, a man followed us up to it and stayed inside the room, watching us as I packed a nightdress, a dressing gown, slippers, a brush and comb and a toothbrush and toothpaste that I found in the bathroom that opened out of the bedroom, into the suitcase that Brian had carried. I did not try to select any of the cosmetics from the array of them on the dressing table. She had not put them on her list. But I added a cardigan that I found lying on a chair, in case she should need it in the morning, and some handkerchiefs. If she suffered any more wild storms of weeping, she might need them, I thought. The man watched me stolidly, and followed us when we went downstairs and along the lane to our gate. He did not leave us until he had seen us go safely in at it.

Visitors had arrived during our absence. Lucille Bird was seated on the sofa, from which she had displaced the retriever, which had gone into a corner of the room to sulk. Kevin, of course, had come with his mother and was sitting beside her. They must have walked up from their house in the heart of the village, as their Mercedes was not in the lane. It did not surprise me to see them there, as Lucille would never want to be left out of a drama. She gave Brian and me a brief nod as we came into the room, but did not interrupt what she was saying.

'. . . fingerprints,' she was saying. 'Of course they'll look for fingerprints. But that's normally useless nowadays. We've all read too much about them in detective stories to know that one should never set out to commit a crime without wearing gloves. Ask Kevin. He's always reading the things. He'll tell you no one would think of committing a murder, or even a burglary, without gloves. Isn't that true, Kevin?'

'Yes, Ma, dear, quite true,' he answered. Her stern, sharp-featured face managed to produce a small smile, as if it were a minor triumph to have induced Kevin to agree with her. In fact, I had never heard him do anything else. But his plump, pink cheeks looked paler than usual and it seemed to me that his air of wilting under her gaze was particularly pronounced.

'I think they've been looking for fingerprints,' I said. 'There was a lot of a greyish sort of dust everywhere. But if they find Fred's fingerprints in the house, it won't mean anything, will it, Avril? Didn't you generally give him a cup of tea when he was working for you. So his prints would be there as a matter of course, at least in the kitchen.'

She gave a heavy sigh. It looked as if she had been crying again while we had been gone. Her face looked drained and blank, with reddened eyelids.

'Yes, I always made him a cup of tea and he'd come in for it and we'd generally sit and have a gossip in the kitchen,' she said. 'But he's been all over the house, doing odd jobs for us at different times. He put a new washer on one of our bathroom taps, and hung a few pictures we'd bought in the drawing room, and mended the electric lamp in the hall when the flex got broken. If it's true that Frances saw him at the gate and he went into the house and murdered Peter, he'd no need to wear gloves.'

'But was this man you saw wearing gloves, Frances?' Lucille asked me, her tone sounding as if she were putting me through an examination.

'I don't think so,' I said. 'I don't know. I didn't notice . . .' But there I stopped, because all of a sudden I seemed to see the man clearly, and something that had been worrying me obscurely about him ever since I had seen him became certain in my mind. He *had* been wearing gloves. And that, in Fred Dyer, had seemed very

66

strange. 'Well, perhaps he was,' I said. 'Really I'm inclined to think so after all.'

'You aren't sure?' Malcolm asked.

'Not a hundred per cent. But I believe he may have been.'

'Then that makes it even less certain that the man at the gate was really Dyer,' Malcolm said. 'As Avril said, he'd have had no need to conceal his fingerprints. But if he was someone else got up to look like Dyer, it could have been important for him to leave no prints behind.'

The doorbell rang.

I went to answer it, expecting more policemen.

But the two people on the doorstep were Fred Dyer and Sharon Sawyer.

'You needn't look so afraid of me,' Fred said. 'I'm not a murderer. Sharon can prove it.'

CHAPTER 4

I took them into the sitting room.

Lucille gave an exclamation that sounded almost like a small scream. Kevin got to his feet and stood looking helpless and bewildered, as if he were waiting for his mother to tell him how to behave. Malcolm and Brian also rose. The Belgian shepherd barked. The retriever growled. The Labrador was too deeply asleep to take any notice of the newcomers.

Malcolm introduced Fred and Sharon to Brian. That Lucille and Kevin knew them he took for granted. But he need not have introduced Fred to Brian. Fred gave him a sardonic smile and said, 'Evening, Mr Hewlett.'

'Evening, Jack,' Brian responded.

'Fred in the present company, if you don't mind,' Fred said.

'It won't make much difference,' Brian said. 'I've told them of our previous acquaintance.'

'I might have known you would. But you haven't had a chance yet to tell it to my girlfriend. Sharon, this gentleman knew me before I came to Raneswood. He can tell you some things about me I've never got around to telling you.'

'Is that true?' Brian asked. 'Have you really not got around to telling the poor girl about your past?'

'Why should I?' Fred asked. 'I came here to get away from it, didn't I? And just what is that past that I should have told her about? That I worked in a garage and that some stories got around about me that I didn't like. You don't need telling, do you, Mr Hewlett, that there was never any evidence against me?'

As usual, his accent was puzzling me. Basically, I felt, it was that of a reasonably well-educated man who had taken pains to cover this fact by a careful imitation of the local accent. It might be the other way about, of course, and that the local accent was natural to him and that he had made an effort to acquire what he thought appropriate for a man of the middle class.

Sharon was looking at him with a shy, puzzled gaze. She was a slim, pretty girl of about twenty-three with a mass of fair, curly hair tied back from her face with a scarlet ribbon, a small, triangular face, wide at the temple, pointed at the chin, with big, earnest blue eyes, a neat little nose and a wide, delicately shaped mouth. She gave the impression of being very diffident and very serious. I wondered how she and Fred had ever become lovers and whether he was her first, or if her appearance of innocence was an illusion.

'Please sit down,' I said, and turned the Labrador firmly out of the chair that he had annexed and pushed another chair up beside it so that they could stay together.

But as I did so, Lucille rose to her feet. After one intimidating glance at the two, she had been careful not to look at them and to act as if she were unaware of their presence.

'Well, Kevin and I will be going home, Frances dear,' she said. 'I don't think we can be of any help to you. But if we can be, of course let me know. Avril, good night. You know you have all our sympathy.'

With nods to Malcolm and Brian but giving no sign that she recognized the existence of Fred and Sharon, unless it was by a slight increase of the hauteur of her usual manner, she took Kevin's arm and swept him out of the room. Fred and Sharon sat down side by side on the sofa that she had abandoned and the Labrador crawled sleepily back into the chair from which I had turned him out.

70

'You'll want to know why we've come,' Fred said. 'It's to straighten out one or two things that we were told by the police. Of course, they've been to see us. They came as soon as they'd been here, I believe, and had a talk with Mrs Chance.' He gave me one of his strange looks at that point that seemed directed straight at me and yet to be looking at something far beyond me. As I had often thought before, there was something very chilling about it. I had never seen any look of warmth on his face, which had always made me feel a certain uneasiness in his presence.

'Forgive me if I'm wrong, Mrs Chance,' he went on, 'but didn't you tell them you saw me at the gate of Mr and Mrs Loxleys' house just a short time before the probable time of the murder?'

'Yes,' I said.

'You said you were sure you saw me there?'

'I said I was fairly sure. When they pressed the point, I admitted I had some doubts.'

'Would you get up in a court of law and swear on oath that it was me you saw?'

'I don't think I would – no.'

'Ah, now that's what I wanted to know. Sharon, tell them where I actually was at the time.'

I was sure it was fear that I saw in her big blue eyes, but there was no tremor in her voice as she spoke. She had a very pleasant voice, low and clear.

'You were having your weekly bath and then you sat by the fire, drinking gin and tonic while I was in the kitchen, making a steak and kidney pudding.'

'And we were able to show the police the remains of the steak and kidney pudding,' Fred said with a grim smile. 'Not that in itself it meant anything. We could have eaten it later than we claimed. But I couldn't have left the flat without Sharon knowing.'

'Did the police believe that?' Brian asked.

71

'Who's to know what the police believe?' Fred asked. 'But people have a way of believing Sharon.'

'Oh, I think they believed me,' Sharon said in her low voice, but still there was a disturbing look of anxiety in her eyes. 'So it couldn't have been Fred that you saw, Mrs Chance.'

'Only someone who wanted to be taken for me,' Fred said.

'And who do you think that might have been?' Brian asked.

Fred gave a harsh little laugh. 'I knew you'd ask me that, Mr Hewlett, and all I can say is that you probably know more about it than I do. Who's about my size and build? Who's got red hair?'

'Or a red wig,' Malcolm suggested.

That brought a short silence into the room, then Avril said hesitantly, 'There's a red wig in the cupboard in the village hall. I mean, where all the costumes we've used for our theatricals are kept. It couldn't be that, could it?'

'Perhaps it could,' Malcolm said. 'And it sounds to me as if it's one of the things we ought to tell the police.'

'But you haven't answered my question,' Fred said. 'Who's about my size and build? Let's say the red hair could have been a wig, but no one's going to say you can get my size and build out of a cupboard.'

'But they aren't so very distinctive,' Malcolm said. 'You're tall and pretty thin and you've got wide shoulders, but I can name several people who fit that description, and dress them up in jeans and a black leather jacket and they could easily be taken for you.'

'Who, for instance?'

That brought another silence and again it was broken by Avril.

'It's a ridiculous thing to think of, because he couldn't look less like Fred, but that description fits Kevin.'

It seemed indeed so ridiculous that I found myself giving a choking little laugh.

72

'All the same, it happens to be true,' Brian said. 'Dress that young man up in the right clothes and a wig and he could just be taken for Dyer.'

'Anyone else?' Fred asked.

'Well, Hugh Maskell for one,' Malcolm said. 'But I'm sure if we worked our way through the village we'd come up with a dozen more. Even the vicar fits the part. So once we've accepted the possibility that the man my wife saw wasn't you, Fred, we're driven back to asking the question, who had a motive to kill Peter Loxley?'

'I was wondering when you'd get to that,' Fred said. 'No one's yet suggested a motive for me. I understand I'm not accused of having stolen anything, and I'm not in love with his wife. What remains is blackmail, and if it was the other way round, that's to say, if it was Loxley who murdered me, not me him, we might have to give it some consideration. But a man with his means isn't going to blackmail the odd-job man.'

It seemed to me that Fred's accent was slipping. He was speaking more and more like the educated man that I was fairly convinced he was.

'Blackmail needn't always be for money,' Brian said. 'Knowledge of another person can be used in all sorts of ways. It can be used simply to wreck a life for the sheer pleasure of doing it. Had Loxley any connections in Edgewater, by any chance?'

A sudden look of fury darkened Fred's face. If he had been alone in the room with Brian I believe he would have assaulted him. As it was, he took one or two deep breaths, then turned to Sharon.

'Come on, love,' he said, 'it's time we were going. We've said what we came to say. We've told Mrs Chance it wasn't me she saw at the gate. There's no point in staying here just to be insulted. Mr Hewlett believes he knows more about me than the police.'

'But I don't understand,' Sharon said, her voice shaking

a little now. 'Why does it matter if Mr Loxley had any connection in Edgewater?'

He put his arm round her shoulders and steered her towards the door.

'I'll tell you when we get home. Let's go now.'

'Yes, but I want to be sure Mrs Chance understands,' Sharon said. 'When she thinks she saw you, you were having a bath, then drinking a gin and tonic, then eating a steak and kidney pudding. It couldn't have been you that she saw.'

In a way it was a pity that she repeated herself, because as she said it the second time it had the sound of something that had been learnt by heart, and not spontaneous, as it had the first time.

Perhaps Fred felt the same, because he seemed all at once in a hurry to leave the room. Malcolm went after them as they went to the front door, and made sure that it was closed behind them.

'So she doesn't know about his doings in Edgewater,' he said as he came back into the room. 'I wonder if he'll really tell her about them when they get home.'

'I wonder how they met in the first place,' Brian said. 'Do you know?'

'No,' Malcolm said, 'but it could easily have been a chance meeting in the old vicarage, where she lives. If he'd been in there, doing a job of work, and she took him out a cup of tea, or something like that. Or it could have been that they picked each other up in a pub, though she doesn't strike me as the kind of girl who'd be in one of them on her own. But it might not have been on her own. She might have been in there with friends and Fred somehow got included in the party. And he'd have been looking for somewhere to stay while he was in Raneswood and might have caught on that she'd take him in if he handled things the right way.'

'Or they might simply have fallen in love with one another,' I said. 'I don't see why you have to assume he was in it for what he could get. Now I'm going to make up the bed for Avril. I'm sorry you're going to be in a very poky little room, Avril, but our one decent spare room is occupied by Brian.'

Of course, Brian immediately offered to move out of it into the poky little room, and of course, Avril refused to let him do it. She came with me when I went upstairs to get the sheets and towels for her, and we made up the bed together in the little room which Malcolm used as a study. It had a divan in it, and an easy-chair, besides the table on which the manuscript of his autobiography was heaped, as well as a typewriter, but there was no dressing table in the room, or any mirror, so I showed her where the bathroom was, with its mirror in a cabinet on the wall. We brought up the suitcase that Brian and I had packed in the house next door, and she assured me that she would be perfectly comfortable.

'It's a pity about the play,' she said. 'She'd have made a charming Juliet.'

We went to bed soon afterwards, though I was not sure how sleepy any of us was. But if we had stayed downstairs together we should only have found ourselves talking endlessly about the events of the day, and I thought that we had all had enough of that. But though I was glad to get into bed, I could not sleep, and after about an hour, realizing that Malcolm was as wakeful as I was, I said, 'Well, is she a liar?'

'Sharon?' he said. 'Yes, I should think so.'

'You don't believe Fred was with her all day?'

'Do you?'

'I don't know. What worries me about her is that she's so frightened of something. It could be just of telling a lie. Or it could be that she's frightened of Fred. I believe I could easily get frightened of him without having any real reason for it. There's something so coldly dominating about him. But that doesn't make her necessarily a liar.'

'Tell me something,' he said. 'How long does it take to make a steak and kidney pudding?'

I was so surprised at the question that I did not answer at once. I wished that I could see Malcolm's face, but it was dark in the room, the faint light of the moon coming through the window showing only the forms of furniture there, and the pallid shape on the pillow that was his face, but not its expression.

'About four hours,' I said.

'Then isn't it possible that during that time he slipped out for a little while without her knowing it?'

'Oh no, because for most of those four hours the pudding is simply steaming quietly and doesn't need any attention paid to it. Actually making it, that's to say making the pastry and lining the bowl with it, and filling it up with the steak and kidney and fixing a cover over it and putting it in a pan to steam takes only a short time. No, she knows what he was doing while she was doing that. Either he was sitting by the fire with his gin and tonic, as she said, or he'd gone out and she knows it.'

'And he's frightened her into lying about it.'

'But was it a lie? Aren't we back to the question of whether or not the man I saw at the Loxleys' gate was Fred? If it was only someone got up to look like him, she could be telling the truth.'

After that I was silent again, worrying at the question that had troubled me all day. After a little while, I said, 'Why should anyone try to look like Fred in particular, instead of anyone else?'

'He's someone none of us knows anything much about, isn't he?' Malcolm said. 'We're ready to be suspicious of him. And we know from Brian that if whoever it was had done a little digging into his past, they'd have come upon the unpleasant business in Edgewater. They'd have found that even if it couldn't be proved that he'd anything to do with the murders there, he isn't a very reputable character. For instance, he's not very faithful to his girlfriends, is he? There was one there who gave him an alibi, whom he appears to have abandoned, and now there's Sharon giving him another.'

'But what could he have had against Peter? Could Peter have had some sort of power over him? For instance, could he have had some proof that Fred really was guilty of those murders?'

'I don't think it's very likely.'

'But what other motive could he have had?'

'What motive could anyone have had? Peter always seemed a fairly harmless person, didn't he?'

'Do you think they could have had some connection before Fred came here. You know the story around the village that Fred's a poet, don't you? And Peter was a publisher. Suppose that somehow brought them into contact?'

I heard Malcolm give what sounded like a chuckle.

'I daresay plenty of poets have felt like murdering plenty of publishers,' he said, 'but I've never heard of one who actually did it.'

'Well then, think of the other people who might have done it. They've got to be tall and thin and broad shouldered, because even if the red hair was a wig, those other things couldn't have been faked.'

'You're absolutely sure of them?'

'Absolutely.'

'Then it might have been me you saw, mightn't it? I fit the description.'

'Oh, Malcolm, do be serious. Anyway, you've got an alibi. You were with Brian, somewhere on the Downs.'

'You're more willing to believe Brian than you are Sharon?'

'Yes, naturally.'

'I suppose it is natural. Poor Sharon. Now whom else have we got? Hugh Maskell is tall and thin and broad shouldered, and so, in his drooping way, is Kevin Bird.'

'If Kevin got suspected, his mother wouldn't hesitate to

give him an alibi. But then there are all the other people in the village whom Peter knew, even if we didn't. You might be able to stir up a witch's broth of motives among them. And that's what the police will probably do in the end. But there's something I wanted to say about Hugh . . .'

As I paused again, Malcolm said, 'Well?'

'I know I've asked you this before, but do you think it's possible that Hugh's in love with Avril?'

It was Malcolm who paused now. I could see that he turned on his side in the bed and that he moved a hand to cover his forehead, a trick he had when he was thinking intensely of anything.

'You mean,' he said at last, 'that if that's so, it would give him a motive for murdering Peter?'

'I don't really think so,' I said, 'but it's something that's crossed my mind. Do you think I'm wrong about his feelings for Avril?'

'What do you think hers are for him?'

'She's never given any sign that I've noticed that she had any.'

'You don't think she'd have been ready to go ahead with a tidy little divorce?'

'Would Peter have been ready for it? Even if she wanted it, he might have been absolutely against it. But, Malcolm, I know there's probably nothing whatever in this idea of mine, and talking about it is just the way rumours with no foundation get started. I wouldn't ever have said anything about it to anyone but you.'

'I think that's wise of you.'

'But I just can't help thinking there might be something in it.'

'All the same, I shouldn't drop a hint of it to the police.'

'Good Lord, what do you take me for?'

'Someone who's a little dangerously perceptive. I wouldn't be at all surprised if you're right.'

'That Hugh's in love with Avril and to get Peter out of

the way when he wouldn't agree to a divorce, he disguised himself as Fred and went in and shot Peter.' I also turned on my side and curled up comfortably, 'I'm glad I talked about it, it's made it sound so absurd. I feel better now. I think I'll get some sleep. Good night, Malcolm.'

'Good night.'

I was asleep in a few minutes. Whether or not Malcolm also fell asleep then I did not know.

Next morning, the house and the garden next door were crawling with policemen. They moved, stooping, in an arc across the lawn and seemed to be examining every particle of dust on the paved path from the gate to the front door. Our telephone rang, and that was a police message that we would be welcome at the police station in Otterswell to sign the statements that we had made the day before. But when Avril said that she would drive into Otterswell in her car, taking the dogs with her, it turned out that the police in charge of her home had no intention of allowing her to remove the car from it, even though it was on police business. So we arranged that she should be driven in with Malcolm and Brian, and that I would remain at home to keep the dogs company, and drive in by myself when the others returned.

Avril was in a strange mood that morning. She had a dishevelled look, almost as if she had been to sleep in her clothes, instead of in what Brian and I had collected for her the evening before. She had not bothered to brush back her smooth fair hair but let it tumble on her shoulders. Her face was haggard and pinched. She drank three cups of coffee, but would eat nothing. When anyone spoke to her, she appeared not to hear it, and then, after an interval in which it seemed natural to suppose that she actually had not heard what had been said, she would make a brief, jerky reply. The dogs seemed to sense that there was something amiss, for they stayed close to her, rubbing themselves against her in what had almost the look of an attempt to console her in a sorrow that they felt themselves.

She, Malcolm and Brian set off for Otterswell soon after breakfast, while I went round the house, doing the usual things like stacking the dishwasher, making beds, running the vacuum cleaner over the sitting room carpet and wandering round doing a little half-hearted dusting. The dogs followed me closely wherever I went, which was not entirely a help. There were some tulips in a bowl in the sitting room which it seemed to me were looking a little tired and I threw them out into the dustbin and went into the garden to pick some more, and it was while I was in the garden that the telephone rang.

I hurried indoors and picked it up.

'Hello,' I said.

'Frances?' said the voice of Jane Kerwood, which I recognized without her having to tell me who was speaking. 'Am I right that Avril's staying with you?'

'Yes,' I said. 'We couldn't leave her to sleep by herself in that house next door. But how did you know?'

'I guessed it more or less when Hugh rang up about the rehearsal being cancelled and told me why. He needn't have done it, because I shouldn't have been at the rehearsal anyway, but I think he wanted to talk. And he said that Avril was with you at the time. Frances, what is she going to do? I mean, is she going to go on staying with you, or go back to that house, or what?'

'We haven't got around to discussing it,' I said. 'She's in a state of shock, I think. I doubt if one could get her to think reasonably about it.'

'But she can't stay with you indefinitely, can she?'

'She's welcome to stay as long as she needs to.'

'Of course. I know you mean that. But I've had an idea. It's just that I've been thinking for some time of taking a lodger. This bungalow is really too big for me, and I've been mulling over the possibility of letting a couple of rooms. Would it help now, do you think, if I were to offer them to her. By the way, is she there with you?'

'No, she's gone to the police station in Otterswell with Malcolm and Brian.'

'Well, would it be a good thing to offer the room to her? She'd be quite independent there, with her own key and all, and she could stay as long as she liked without the feeling that she was imposing on anybody. She could cook for herself and pay me whatever we agreed on. Is it a good idea?'

'It sounds to me a splendid idea,' I said, 'but you'll have to get hold of her and discuss it with her. I'd sooner not say anything about it myself, because it might give her the feeling that I want to get her out of the house and have persuaded you to make the offer. If you like, when she gets back, I'll tell her you rang and wanted to speak to her, but I'd better leave the rest to you.'

'Very well; do that. And Frances . . .'

'Yes?'

'Is it true that you saw the murderer?'

News travels very fast in a village.

'Who told you that?' I asked.

'Hugh again. And he'd got it from one of the policemen, I gathered. But is it true?'

'I can't possibly tell, Jane,' I answered. 'I saw someone, and I thought I recognized him, but I'm not even sure of that now. And later I heard a shot, but it may not have been the shot that killed poor Peter.'

'Poor Peter?'

'Yes, well, certainly poor Peter. Aren't you sorry for him?'

'If someone would do to me what they did to him, I'd be very satisfied.'

'Ah, because of that broken heart of yours.'

'Of course.'

'The trouble is, you know, you don't look like a case of a broken heart.'

'You think it ought to show?'

'Certainly.'

'Well, I must give that some thought. I'm not sure if I want everyone noticing it. You're the only person I've told about it. Poor Peter. Yes, I agree, poor Peter, but not for the reason you meant. He was a very unhappy man, did you know that? He couldn't have the one thing he wanted. Goodbye now. You'll tell Avril to call me, won't you?'

She rang off.

As happened only too often after a talk with Jane, I was left irritatingly puzzled. I felt that she wanted to confide in me, that she was trying to tell me something important, but that she always drew back just before she had actually done so. I wondered about the relationship between her and Peter. Whatever it had been, she seemed to be trying to turn it into a wry kind of joke. Anyway, it could not have soured her feelings for Avril, since she was ready to help her now.

I went into the kitchen and started to peel some potatoes.

But I did not get very far with them because before I was half done there was a ring at the doorbell and it was Hugh. His strong-featured face which was normally grave, was even more melancholy than usual. The lines in it seemed more marked.

Coming in, he said, 'I met the others in Otterswell and Malcolm told me I'd find you at home. Aren't you going to Otterswell yourself?'

'Yes, when they get back,' I answered. 'Avril was worried about leaving the dogs alone, so I stayed behind for the present. Have you had to sign a statement for the police?'

I took him into the sitting room.

'Yes, among a dozen or so other people,' he said. 'It seemed to me half the village was there. I saw Avril. She appeared to be in a daze. How is she, Frances? Is there anything one can do for her?'

'Well, she can stay here as long as she likes, and Jane rang up this morning to say she'll let her a room in her bungalow if that would help,' I said. 'I think it might. Did the police just get you to sign a statement, or were there a lot more questions you had to answer?'

'Oh, a lot,' he said, 'though mainly it was simply a repetition of what they asked me yesterday. I suppose to see if I'd slip up in some way and tell them a different story. As it was, there was really only one thing of interest I had to tell them and that was that Peter once showed me the gun that apparently killed him. The one they found beside him. It was his all right. I don't know where or when he got it, but he showed it to me some weeks ago. He was rather proud of it. But he didn't say if he'd any ammunition for it.'

I had sat down and gestured to him to do so too, but he remained standing on the hearth-rug.

'But if the gun was his . . .' I began uncertainly.

'I know,' he said. 'It could be that it was he who tried to shoot whoever it was who'd come in, and that the person grabbed it and there was a struggle and it was Peter who got killed. But the inspector said there were no signs of a struggle.'

'It could have happened like that though, couldn't it?'

'Oh yes, I understood they haven't ruled it out.'

'But it would change the motive they have to look for. If someone came there, perhaps assuming Peter would be in London with Avril and meaning to steal what he could, then got caught by Peter who threatened him with a gun, we needn't look for someone with any real relationship with Peter. For instance, it could be . . .' I paused. I had nearly said it could be Fred Dyer, only I no longer felt at all sure that the man I had seen at the gate had been Fred.

'I like your theory,' Hugh said with a grim sort of smile. 'It lets me off the hook. I had a quite close relationship with Peter, and, as it happens, with Avril too. Some kind neighbour had been telling the police about that.'

'About you and Avril?' I said with embarrassment.

'Yes, the inspector put it to me – was I in love with Avril? He almost stated it as a fact that I was. And so I disguised myself as Dyer and went into the house and somehow got hold of Peter's gun and shot him.' He gave a brief laugh. 'I don't think he actually believed it for a minute. He was trying it out to see if he could get me to talk.'

'And did it?'

'No, it didn't! But tell me something, Frances. Have you come across a lot of people in the neighbourhood who believe that?'

I could feel my cheeks flushing. I knew that they had turned red, and I could see that Hugh had noticed it.

'So that's what you really came in for this morning,' I said. 'To ask me that.'

'Well, don't you want to answer it?'

I shrank from doing so, but said, 'I'll try to tell you the truth, Hugh. I've come across a few people in the neighbourhood who, so far as I know, believe it. And I've been inclined to believe it myself, and I've talked about it to Malcolm. That's all.'

'I see.'

I was not sure what he saw, so I said nothing.

He gave another harsh little laugh. 'I may as well tell you the truth too, I suppose. You're quite right. If Avril hadn't been married, I'd have done my best to get her to marry me. But that doesn't mean I was ready to murder her husband to get her. I don't even know if she'd have wanted me. I've never tried to talk to her about it. And now I don't know what to do. It can't be the right time to speak of such a thing to her, and yet you never know, it might be consoling for her to know that there's someone who wants her.'

'Don't you think she knows that already?'

84

'Do you think so?'

'Well, if a mere observer like me stumbled on the truth, don't you think it's probable that she's known it from the first?'

'Yes. Yes, I see what you mean. All the same, I think it would be a mistake to bring it into the open now.'

'Oh, if you're thinking what the police would make of it, it would certainly be a mistake.'

'You don't mean to tell them about it yourself then?'

'Hugh, what do you take me for?'

'I'm sorry, I shouldn't have said that. I'll be off home now. Thank you for listening to me. I hope the police don't give you a bad time. You and Mrs Henderson are the only witnesses who have anything significant to tell them. Goodbye, my dear.'

He stooped and gave me a light kiss on my forehead, then went out of the room.

I left him to let himself out of the house, then went back to peeling the potatoes.

When Malcolm, Brian and Avril returned, I set off for Otterswell myself. But before I left, I heard Brian take possession of the telephone and from the odd bits of what he was saying that I overheard, I knew that he was talking to Judy, telling her all that had been happening to him in the place to which he had come for peace and quiet. He was still talking as I left the house, and I reflected that it was going to be a very expensive call.

I thought about Hugh as I drove; thinking it was probable that whatever his intention might be at the moment, he would be pouring his heart out to Avril by the evening. I also thought about the fact that although I had told him the literal truth that I had heard no one actually discussing his feelings for Avril, I had heard hints dropped, had noticed glances and raised eyebrows and the occasional smile which had shown that a number of people had thought as I had about their relationship. In fact, it had been these things that had made me think about the situation myself. What I knew nothing about were Avril's feelings for Hugh. I had been fairly sure that the Loxleys' marriage was not a happy one, but I had had no reason to believe that Hugh was the cause of it.

In Otterswell I drove to the police station, parked the car, went inside and introduced myself and asked for Detective Inspector Holroyd. I was taken into a small, depressingly bare, virtually unfurnished room and the inspector, together with the sergeant who had been with him the day before, followed me into it almost immediately. Once the inspector was there, the room no longer seemed empty. His bulk seemed to fill the place all by itself. We sat down facing one another across a table and the sergeant squeezed himself into the little space that was left at one end of it, produced papers which I assumed were the statement I would have to sign, and another notebook. The inspector offered me a cigarette and when I refused gave a sigh, as if the increasing number of witnesses and suspects who would not smoke somehow diminished his sense of authority.

'Well now, Mrs Chance, this needn't take us long,' he said. 'But I'd like to go over one or two of the things you told us yesterday. This man, Fred Dyer, whom you saw at the Loxleys' gate –'

'I'm not at all sure it was Fred Dyer,' I interrupted, then had a feeling that I had done exactly what he wanted. 'Didn't I say that yesterday? The more I think of it, the more I feel it was someone who'd made himself up to look like Fred.'

'Would you go so far as to say you're sure of that?'

'Almost,' I said. 'His hair was wrong. It was longer than Fred wears his, and it wasn't the right colour – well, I think it wasn't. But still, I can't say I'm absolutely certain. When I passed him in the lane it never occurred to me it was anyone but Fred. I only thought there was something wrong about the way he acted, keeping turned away from me and not chatting at all. That did strike me as unlike him.'

'You'd say then that Fred Dyer is normally a friendly man,' the inspector said.

'No, I don't think I would. I think he's pretty stand-offish. But he isn't discourteous. He'd sooner say he thought it was probably going to rain presently, or something like that, than intentionally cut one dead.'

'And there were the gloves, of course.'

'Yes, the gloves. I'm sure he was wearing them.'

'You don't believe it was Dyer you saw, do you?'

We gave each other a long look without saying anything. The fact that he was putting pressure on me to say that it had not been Fred Dyer at the gate made me determined not to commit myself. Yet the trouble was that he was right about my feelings.

'I'm sorry I can't really help you,' I said. 'I liked Peter Loxley, you know. I'd like you to catch his murderer.'

'Well now, suppose you take a look at this statement that Sergeant Miles has here,' he said, apparently giving up the attempt to get a really definite answer out of me, 'and if you're satisfied that it's an accurate version of what you told us yesterday, sign it for us.' He handed me a couple of sheets of paper.

The statement was admirably accurate and I signed it, then was told that that was all that was wanted of me. I went out to the car and drove home. I tried to think of other things besides the murder, for instance of Hugh being in love with Avril and never telling her so, and of Jane Kerwood's broken heart and who had managed to break it. But these things did not really seem dissociated from the murder. For one thing, I did not know whether or not to believe what either of them had told me, and though each might have a reason for invention that had nothing to do with the murder, but only with private troubles and heartache of their own, it somehow seemed likely that lies were being told at the moment which were somehow connected with the mystery of Peter Loxley's death. I reached home and put the car in the garage, then started up the path to the front door.

But I had taken only a step or two when I saw a very extraordinary thing. Someone was sitting on our doorstep. A woman. A woman whom for a moment I took to be Avril. She had Avril's fair hair drawn back austerely from her oval face, her wide-spaced blue eyes and delicate features. And there was a look of casual grace about the way she sprawled on the doorstep of which Avril might have been capable if it had ever occurred to her to sit there. But she was not Avril, though I knew her face almost as well as Avril's. It was her cousin, Lynne Denison.

CHAPTER 5

She got to her feet as I came up the path. Standing, she looked a little less like Avril. She was not as tall and she was even slimmer and there was something more alive, more expressive about her face.

'So it was worth waiting,' she observed as I joined her by the door. 'I thought someone would turn up sooner or later.'

Her voice was quite different from Avril's. It was richer and warmer.

'Have you been waiting long?' I asked.

'No, only a few minutes,' she said. 'I came by taxi from Otterswell, and I let it go before I was sure there was anyone at home. By the way, I'm Avril Loxley's cousin, Lynne Denison.'

I smiled. 'I knew that. And I'm Frances Chance and I live here. Is there really no one at home?'

'Well, I've tried ringing and knocking and I've been round to the back to see if I could get in there; in fact, I've tried everything but shouting, but there's been no response.'

I took my key out of my handbag. 'Let's go in then, and see if we can find out what's happened to everybody.'

I unlocked the door and pushed it open and led the way inside. Picking up a small suitcase that she had with her, Lynne followed me. I did not know what I expected to find, but I had a frightened sort of feeling that there might be some sort of horror waiting for us. That was what the events of the last twenty-four hours had done to me. I did not fear anything in particular, but the mere emptiness of the house when I was expecting several people to be there gave me a feeling of tingling apprehension.

In fact, the house was empty. Nothing was out of place. The potatoes that I had peeled were still in their bowl in the kitchen sink. The copy of *The Times* that Brian had been reading when I left for Otterswell was in a fairly crumpled state on the sofa where he had been sitting. There was a slight warmth in the room, as if the electric fire on the hearth had only recently been switched off.

'Just wait a minute,' I said to Lynne. 'I don't know where everyone's got to, but I'll take a look upstairs.'

But there was no one upstairs.

Coming down, I said, 'No, they've all gone out. I expect Avril had to take the dogs for a walk, and my husband and a friend who's staying with us have also gone for a walk. Of course, it was Avril you came to see. You know – do you? About Peter?'

She was standing in the middle of the sitting room, looking round her, taking in her surroundings. I had a feeling that that was something that she would always do. The scene in which she found herself would always be a matter of importance to her.

'One could hardly help it if one watched the television news last night,' she said.

'Ah yes, of course,' I said. 'We didn't watch it.'

'I expect you had too much else to think about. But I saw it and I thought I'd come down to see if I could help Avril. Things must be terrible for her. Not that there's anything special I can think of that I can do for her, though I might take her back to London with me. I suppose she'll have to stay here till after the inquest, but then perhaps she'd like to come. And I thought she might even come back to Hollywood with me. What do you think?'

'There'd be the problem of her dogs,' I said. 'She's got three dogs, all rather large. I don't know if she told you that.'

'Oh yes, those dogs. She did tell me about them. But couldn't she board them in some kennels somewhere?'

'I dare say she could if someone persuaded her to do it. Now what about some sherry? May I give you some?'

'Thank you, yes.'

I went to the cupboard to get out the bottle and glasses.

'But how did you know she'd be staying here?' I asked.

'From a policeman next door,' she answered. 'The taxi actually put me down there, and I could see that there were several policemen in the house. So I asked one if he knew where Mrs Loxley was and he said to the best of his knowledge she was staying here.' She took the glass I had given her and sat down in a chair near the fire which I had just switched on. 'Am I terribly in the way? Do please go ahead with anything you meant to do. For the moment, this drink is all I need.'

I sat down in a chair facing her. 'I don't know what there's any point in doing as I don't know where everybody is. I don't know how many people I'm supposed to be cooking for.'

'Oh, don't cook for anyone,' she said. 'Come down and have lunch at the Green Man with me. I booked in there on my way here. If the others have come home before we go, they can come with us; and if they haven't got back, you can leave a message for them telling them where to join us. By the way, what literate taxi-drivers you have. When I said I wanted to be taken to Raneswood, he didn't say, "Oh, that's where they've had a murder." He said, "That's where they're doing a production of *Romeo and Juliet*, isn't it?" Then to my surprise, he said that he didn't like Shakespeare. I thought that was awfully brave of him. After all, everyone *has* to like Shakespeare; you can't say you don't.'

'Did he recognize you?'

'I don't think so; or if he did, he was too polite to say so. After all, he might not like me. Not everybody does.

Frances, about those dogs of Avril's, are they really and truly hers, or were they actually Peter's?'

'D'you know, I've never asked myself that question,' I said. 'I've always taken for granted they were hers. In fact, that they were her substitute for not having had children.'

'You never wondered if they were Peter's substitute?'

It was a fact that I had never done so. She was watching me with something peculiarly intent in her blue eyes, it might almost have been something mocking. I had a feeling that she was taking me for some kind of simpleton and I did not much like the feeling.

'I don't think I know what you mean,' I said. 'Did Peter want children very badly?'

'Avril's never talked to you about that?' she said.

'No.'

She looked down into her glass of sherry and I was glad to be freed from her searching stare.

'And of course you've always taken for granted that their failure to have children was Avril's fault,' she said. 'But it wasn't, you know, it was Peter's.'

'You mean he refused to have them?'

'No, no, simply that he couldn't. At first, when a child didn't come, they took for granted it was something wrong with Avril, and she went to I don't know how many doctors to see if it could be put right. But they all said there was nothing the matter with her and that she was perfectly normal. So at last it was Peter who started going to doctors and the answer was that it was he who couldn't have children. There was nothing wrong with him sexually, you understand, but he was – I suppose the word's sterile. Avril told me all that at lunch yesterday and I expect I shouldn't be handing it all on to you, but now that Peter's dead I somehow can't keep it to myself. I don't mean that it's got anything to do with the murder, but I think Avril may need a friend who knows the truth about what she's been going through. She was so loyal to him when he couldn't give her the one thing she wanted.'

92

Those words roused a curious echo in my mind. It was of Jane Kerwood saying to me that Peter had been an unhappy man because he couldn't have the one thing in life he wanted. But had she meant simply that he could not have a child, or had it been that he had been unable to give Avril the one thing that would make her happy? Had he feared that sooner or later she was likely to leave him?

Wondering if it had been from him that Jane had learnt the truth about the Loxleys' relationship, or if it had been from Avril, I said, 'It's a very sad story.'

'It just happens that for Peter and Avril it was,' Lynne said. 'For some people it wouldn't have mattered so very much. I've always been thankful that I haven't had children, but then I'm not very clever at choosing husbands, and children would have complicated things so much. You see, I think that once you've got them you've got to put them first. You don't know what I've seen in Hollywood of children going wrong out of the sheer missing of that in so-called one-parent families. Or perhaps I mean too many parents, who keep changing. But you've no children yourself, have you? Has it mattered to you very much?'

'I suppose it did for a while long ago,' I answered. 'But Malcolm was really all I ever wanted . . . Oh, I think they're here.' For I had heard the squeak our gate always gave when it was opened and footsteps on the path to the house. I went on hurriedly, 'Are you planning to tell the police what you've just told me about Peter, Lynne?'

'Good heavens, no!' she exclaimed. 'It can't have anything to do with his murder. And you won't tell them either, will you?'

I heard myself promising not to, but with a feeling that to bind myself in any way just then as to what I told anyone about anything was a mistake. Lynne had certainly been talking too much, telling me what had been told to her in confidence, but that did not seem to have occurred to her. I thought that probably she would tell it all to the next person with whom she found herself alone.

The door opened and Malcolm and Brian came in.

I introduced Lynne and they expressed great pleasure at seeing her, wanted to know, as I had, what had brought her, and heard of her learning about Peter's murder from television. Then they helped themselves to sherry and Malcolm said that of course Lynne was staying for lunch.

'Oh no, you're all coming down to have lunch with me at the Green Man,' she said. 'But tell me, where's Avril?'

'And where have you been?' I asked.

'Only for a bit of a walk,' Malcolm said. 'We thought we'd get home before you got back from Otterswell.'

'We both felt an overpowering desire to go somewhere where we wouldn't be able to see a single policeman,' Brian said. 'We've been up on the Downs.' He was looking at Lynne with deep interest, as if she were of a species that he had never encountered before. Yet Granborough parents were such a mixed lot that I was sure he must have met and entertained at least a few actors and actresses, some of them almost as famous as Lynne, as Malcolm and I had in our time. 'I realize we ought to have left a note for you to tell you where we'd gone,' he went on. 'I'm sorry if you were worried.'

'I wasn't specially worried about you two,' I said, 'but as Lynne just asked you, where's Avril?'

'She went to call in on Jane,' Malcolm answered. 'Jane's had the idea that Avril might move in with her as a lodger, at least for a time. Avril seemed to like the idea. And she set off to discuss it with her, of course taking the dogs. It's very kind of you to invite us to the Green Man, Mrs Denison, but I think we ought to wait till Avril gets back.'

'Lynne,' she said.

'Lynne,' he responded with a smile. 'Though I could try phoning Jane to see if Avril's started back already, and if she hasn't, I could tell her perhaps to meet us at the Green Man.'

'Yes, do that,' Lynne said.

Malcolm went out to the telephone in the hall and I heard him speak for a minute or two, presumably to Jane, but when he came back into the room he shook his head.

'She's left Jane already, so we'll have to wait for her,' he said. 'She should be here in a few minutes.'

As he spoke, I heard the squeak of the gate, and a moment later Avril came into the room with the three dogs thrusting their way in ahead of her, and scenting a stranger in Lynne, investigating her with a mixture of hesitant growling and little yelps of pleasure.

As soon as she saw Lynne, Avril threw herself into her arms. The two of them clung together, and tears began to stream from Avril's eyes.

'Oh, Lynne, you shouldn't have . . . You can't do anything . . . You can't help . . . It's all so awful, but you shouldn't have come.' The broken sentences came from Avril between choking sobs. 'But I'm so glad to see you.'

'I know I can't do anything, but I couldn't think of you here alone,' Lynne said. 'I know you've got good friends, but it isn't the same thing. Now, we're going out to lunch at the Green Man. You've got to face other people sooner or later, so we may as well get it over now, or would you really very much sooner stay here?'

Avril withdrew from the embrace of her cousin and mopped her eyes.

'No, let's go.'

I thought of my uselessly peeled potatoes in the bowl in the kitchen sink, but on the whole was glad that I had no need to go on and prepare the rest of the meal. Avril at first was unsure what she should do with the dogs, but with a little persuasion from Malcolm, decided to have them tied on their leads to a pole in the garden that was used for supporting the line that took the washing. Their whines of protest followed us as we set off down the lane.

Avril and Lynne went ahead, talking quietly and confidentially to one another. Brian chose to walk by himself.

Malcolm and I stayed a few yards behind them. At first, while we were passing the police cars, we were silent. I wanted to talk, to tell Malcolm what Lynne had told me about Peter, but I remembered that I had promised not to tell this to the police, and I was not sure if that really meant strictly the police or if it included everyone else as well. But I thought that anyone who knew us would know that Malcolm and I were one identity, that we had no secrets from one another, and that telling one of us something was the same as telling it to us both. Not that Lynne knew us, but I felt she ought to have taken it for granted.

With my arm through his, I said, 'Malcolm, Lynne told me a rather surprising thing before you got home.' And I went on and told him what she had told me of Peter's inability to father a child.

He was less interested than I had thought he would be.

'I don't know what that woman's come here for,' he muttered. 'It'll only bring the press down on us. Is that why she came, d'you think? Did she think that being connected with a murder would be useful publicity?'

'I should have thought it would be very bad publicity,' I said.

'You can't tell nowadays,' he said. 'Haven't you noticed how the news on television, night after night, consists of violence of some sort or other. Civil wars, terrorism, riots, assassinations, road accidents and probably a homely murder or two, like ours. Good news isn't news, apparently, or does nothing good ever actually happen? I wish she hadn't come.'

'But I'm sure it was just out of good nature,' I said. 'You could see how glad Avril was to see her.'

'Avril started life as an actress, didn't she, even though she never got anywhere with it?'

I looked at him in surprise.

'D'you mean you didn't believe she was glad to see Lynne?'

'I felt a touch of doubt.'

96

'But why?'

'I don't know, I don't know,' he said irritably. 'It was just a feeling I had for a moment. Probably quite wrong. But what you've been telling me about Peter doesn't really have any connection with the murder, does it? You might say, I suppose, that it gave Avril a possible motive for killing him, but wouldn't a divorce and remarriage really have done as well? Or she could simply have left him and found herself a boyfriend.'

'Yes, she could have left him,' I said, 'but she may have been worried about money. Except for that attempt to be an actress, I don't think she's ever had any sort of job and I don't suppose he'd have kept her supplied if she'd simply walked out on him. He may have refused a divorce, and I don't suppose he'd ever given her grounds for going ahead with one on her own, so I don't believe he'd have had to pay her anything. But now that he's dead I suppose she'll inherit all he had – his share of that company Loxley Matthews, for instance.'

'Anyway, she was in London when he was killed, so she can't have had anything to do with it.'

'Of course.'

He gave me a sidelong look.

'Are you really beginning to get suspicious of her, Frances?'

'I'm a little bit suspicious of almost everybody, I find, and at the same time nobody. Oh, I don't know what I think, and I don't suppose you do either. I'd like to think about something quite different – those celandines, for instance.'

They were in the grass at the base of the hedgerow down the other side of the lane, gaily yellow and full of the spring. On the other side of the lane, where the houses were, we had passed the cottage where the two sisters lived, and who at that time were in the South of France, so there was no sign of life there. But in the garden of the next house, where the Askews, the young couple with the two small children lived, the whole family was out, doing some weeding of the flowerbeds, and also keeping an eye on what was going on in the Loxleys' garden. When they saw us they waved to us and we waved back. They had not been in the village very long and we did not know them well, though we had been for drinks in each other's houses and I liked what I knew of them. But now a curious thing happened. The young man, Ernest Askew, who had been stooping over a bed of wallflowers, plucking out weeds, straightened up and stood for a moment, rubbing his back as if it were aching and I saw that he was wearing gardening gloves. I also saw that he was tall, slim, well-built and wide-shouldered, and for a moment, I had a singular vision of him as red-haired, when in fact his thick, curly hair was a dark brown. But with a red wig covering the dark brown, he could quite easily have been the figure that I had seen at the Loxleys' gate, which I had taken for Fred Dyer.

It was only momentary. I had no reason to imagine that Ernest Askew would shoot Peter Loxley. Yet he could so easily have been the man at the gate. And for all I knew, he and Peter might have had some violent quarrel. But I had no reason either to imagine that Fred Dyer would shoot Peter, and I realized that if I was not careful I should be seeing possible Fred Dyers everywhere. As we walked on, I tried very hard to recall exactly what that figure at the gate had been like. *Had* it been Fred? There had been something wrong, it seemed to me now, about the red hair. It had been a little too brilliantly red and a little too thick and bushy, in fact, just the sort of hair that someone wearing the wig from the cupboard in the village hall would have appeared to have. The more I thought about it, the more convinced of this I became, but I did not speak of it to Malcolm. I would tell Detective Inspector Holroyd about it when next I saw him, which I supposed would be fairly soon. We walked on past Hugh Maskell's house and into the road that wound through the village. Hugh was tall, well-built and wide-shouldered and just possibly had a motive . . . I did my best not to think of that as we approached the Green Man.

It was a long, gabled building, mostly covered in cream-coloured rough-cast and built in Victorian times. It had a large car park behind it and next to it, with only a narrow alley between them, was a pleasant-looking modern house with a roof of grey pantiles and painted a pale green, in which Lucille and Kevin Bird lived. It was Kevin's work and fairly successful. There was a narrow strip of lawn in front of it, with no fence between it and the road. The very handsome garden that Lucille had created was at the back of the house. She and Kevin were just coming out of it and making their way to the entrance of the Green Man as we approached.

Malcolm introduced Lynne to them and she gave them the smile that had enchanted thousands. Kevin looked as if he would have wagged his tail if he had had a tail to wag. Lucille greeted her stiffly.

'We are honoured,' she said gravely, the pleasure she took in meeting a celebrity evident in her tone. She led the way in at the door. The room inside was long with a bar at one end of it, and several mirrors and framed advertisements hung on the walls. A number of the tables were placed close together and a good many of these had been taken so that the place already seemed full. 'You'll join us,' Lucille stated. 'Kevin and I often come in here for Sunday lunch.'

None of the tables was big enough to take seven people, but we pushed two together and seated ourselves on benches round them.

'Their steak and chips is really very creditable,' Lucille went on. 'But what will you have to drink? Kevin, you'll get us our drinks. Mrs Denison, you must be quite American by now; you'd like a cocktail, I'm sure, but I advise you against anything more ambitious than a gin and tonic.

Or would you prefer whisky? Scotch on the rocks, what about that? . . . No? Sherry? Frances, I know you will have sherry and Malcolm will have whisky and water without ice. Mr Hewlett, what will you have?'

Brian chose whisky with water without ice, and as Kevin set off to the bar to collect the drinks, Brian followed him to help him bring them to the table. Lucille herself and Kevin both had sherry. By the time that Kevin and Brian returned to the table, a young woman in jeans and a T-shirt had planted a menu on our table and left us, and when she came back to take our orders, we all seemed to feel that Lucille had decided what we were to eat and obediently asked for steak and chips, though I have a liking for fish and chips myself, as they do them at the Green Man, but I lacked the courage not to conform.

Looking at Lynne with stiff graciousness, Lucille said, 'You've chosen an unfortunate time to come to Raneswood, Mrs Denison. You must be finding the atmosphere very different from what you expected.'

'Oh, I knew what had happened here before I came,' Lynne answered. 'In fact, it was what brought me. I thought I might be able to take Avril back to London with me. But she seems to have managed to make arrangements here for herself.'

'I'm so glad that Kevin and I are getting away,' Lucille said. 'Did I tell you about our plans to go to my relatives in Toronto? We're going next week. I'm so looking forward to it. They're always so good to me. Last time I went, about a year ago, Kevin couldn't go with me, as he hadn't got leave from his office, but this time we've arranged things so that the visit coincides with his holiday. You're very pleased about that, aren't you, Kevin? Kevin loves Canada.'

At that moment, a man with a camera aimed it at Lynne and rapidly snapped a photograph of her. She seemed unconscious of it, as she did when another man did the same, unless a certain air of sadness about her, that appeared to me to increase just then, was her response to it. It might have been that she thought this appropriate to her situation, rather than the almost cheerful face with which she had listened to Lucille. I was afraid that these men might be going to intrude on our lunch party with questions to Lynne, but they had the courtesy not to do so.

A few minutes later, when our steak and chips was just being served to us, Fred Dyer and Sharon Sawyer came into the bar.

They made for a table at the far end of the room, and in passing us, Sharon gave us a shy little smile, and Fred a stiff nod without a trace of a smile on his face. When they sat down, Fred had his back to us and his broad shoulders blotted out Sharon from our view. All of us except Lynne had nodded back to them as they passed, then acted as if we had no special interest in them, but Lynne gazed after them with a look of astonishment on her face.

'Who is that perfectly gorgeous man?' she asked.

It took me by surprise. I had never thought of Fred as gorgeous. But his air of remoteness, that trick he had of looking through one as if he did not really recognize one's existence, had always put me off. I knew that in appreciating people's looks I was more likely to be influenced by the expression on their faces, rather than by their features, and Fred's expression had none of the warmth and liveliness that I liked. But trying to see him now with Lynne's eyes, I had to admit that his features were excellent. If you did not care too much about what his face told you about him, he really was very good-looking.

Brian responded to Lynne. 'That gorgeous man is very likely a multiple murderer.'

She gave a smothered little cry and Lucille said, 'What *do* you mean, Mr Hewlett?'

He gave a shrug. 'I shouldn't have said that. Forget it.'

'No, but you must have meant something,' Lucille said.

'I know there's some suspicion that he may have been connected with poor Peter's death, but a *multiple* murderer – what can you mean?'

'As I said, I shouldn't have said it,' Brian replied, though I felt fairly sure that he had done it deliberately, for reasons of his own. 'But the truth is, every time I see him, I find myself wondering what he's doing in Raneswood. He worked for a time in Edgewater, you see, where I live myself, and he left it because he found himself being suspected of having committed three particularly revolting murders. You no doubt remember them. Three girls were found strangled, with their heads smothered in black plastic bags, and a woman claimed to have seen Fred Dyer, or Jack Benyon as we called him then, leaving the spot where one of the bodies was found – '

'Oh, please, please,' Kevin broke in, his voice unnaturally shrill, 'don't go on with it! I can't stand it. I'll never be able to eat my steak and chips if you go on.'

'Don't be ridiculous, dear boy,' Lucille said. 'I find this very interesting. You say he was called Jack Benyon when he was in Edgewater, Mr Hewlett. You're quite sure of that?'

'Yes, quite sure,' Brian replied. 'He may or may not be a murderer, but he's some kind of crook. People don't change their names for nothing.'

'But he wasn't arrested?'

'No, there wasn't nearly enough evidence against him. The woman who identified him changed her mind and his girlfriend gave him an alibi. But then he disappeared. That seemed to tell against him, but actually, he'd told our Inspector Dalling, who was in charge of the case, that he was going, and why. And I suppose his reason was a perfectly good one, that he couldn't stand the atmosphere of suspicion in which he was living. I think most people thought he was guilty. But I'd like to know what brought him to Raneswood. Was it just chance, or did he come here for some reason?'

'What reason could he possibly have?' Lucille asked. 'I suppose he was just drifting about, getting jobs where he could, and then he happened to pick up with that girl, Sharon, and she gave him a place to live and no doubt introduced him to people she knew who gave him jobs and he found he could make a living.'

Lynne leant forward.

'But you've some idea in your mind, haven't you, Mr Hewlett?' she said.

'An idea?' he said.

'An idea about a reason that could have brought him here.'

'Not really. No.'

'I think you have.'

He shook his head. 'One has fancies, but I think Mrs Bird's probably right, that he drifted here by chance.'

At that moment, Fred got up and went to the bar to get himself and Sharon more drinks and I had the first clear view of her that I had had since they had sat down and if ever I had seen fear on a human face, there it was. There was an agony of anxiety in her eyes. Then she leant back in her chair, closing them, as if she felt that they were betraying her. She looked very young and forlorn. I felt a disagreeable twinge of guilt, because it was almost certainly my identifying Fred as the man whom I had seen at the Loxleys' gate that now filled her with terror. Whether it was terror of what might happen to him, or of the man himself, I could not tell. If it was of what might happen to him it must mean that the alibi that she had given him was false and that she herself believed in my identification and that she was living with a murderer. But more probably it was fear that he would be unable to prove his innocence and at any time now might be arrested, what she had to say for him simply not being believed. I wondered if I could get hold of her and tell her that I was almost sure now that I had been mistaken in thinking that it was Fred whom I had seen at the gate.

Fred returned to their table with a couple of whiskies and his broad shoulders blotted out her face again, but the memory of it stayed with me. I would have to do something about it, I realized. I could not leave her in that state of misery.

Lucille was talking to Avril, 'Perhaps it's wrong of me to ask you such a thing here, Avril, dear, but have you made any plans for your future? It must be a terribly difficult time for you and if there's any way that Kevin and I can help you, you must tell us. Of course, I don't suppose there is. So often in life one has this desire to help, and actually there's nothing whatever one can do, but you must remember we're friends.'

'You're very kind,' Avril said in a low voice. 'But actually, I've made what I think is a very good arrangement for the immediate future. I'm moving in with Jane as a lodger. I know that Frances would let me stay on as long as I liked, but I feel I'm imposing on her, whereas with Jane it's a business arrangement which will be beneficial to us both. But I don't suppose I shall stay with her for very long. I think I shall go to London. We've a flat there and I can just move in without any trouble. And perhaps, when I'm feeling more normal, I'll look for a job. I might even look for something at Loxley Matthews. I always took an interest in Peter's work there, and they might find something I could do.'

'But what about your dogs?' Lucille asked. 'You can't take them to a flat in London.'

'Oh, I'll have to have them put down,' Avril answered.

She said it casually, as if the animals which had seemed for the last year or two to have been the centre of her life were of no importance to her. I looked at her face. It was very pale and expressionless and I realized that probably she hardly knew what she was saying.

Kevin seemed to feel the same. 'You can't mean that. Those lovely creatures. Of course you don't mean it. If you really want to get rid of them, you can sell them, or even give them away to friends. Ma and I would take the Belgian shepherd.'

'I couldn't do that,' Avril said in her new flat, matter-of-fact voice. 'They're mine. It would feel like giving a bit of myself away.'

'But it's cruel,' Kevin said, 'killing them.'

'I hate to hear it called killing,' Avril responded. 'They'll be put down. It's quite painless.'

'You don't mind having a bit of yourself put down?' Brian said. 'You won't give it away, but you don't mind killing it. Because, after all, it is killing.'

I saw the stubborn look come on to her face, which I had sometimes seen there before. It made it look uncommonly hard. But there was something else about it that troubled me, though I could not make out what it was. It reminded me of something, though I could not think for the moment of what. It was something that I had seen somewhere, but where or when it had been eluded me.

We finished our lunch mostly in silence, though Lucille made several rather brave attempts at starting a conversation. Afterwards, as we left, we had to run the gauntlet of the press. They had gathered outside the Green Man, waiting for Lynne. She dealt with them with professional skill, assuring them that her arrival had nothing to do with the murder but was purely to spend a little time with a cousin of hers. To direct questions she answered, 'No comment'. Lucille and Kevin left us and went to their house. The rest of us started the walk back to our house.

When we reached the Loxleys' house it looked as if the police had left it. Avril stood still at the gate.

'D'you know, I think I'll go in and pack a couple of suitcases to take to Jane's,' she said. 'She said I could move in as soon as I liked, and I hate the feeling of being a nuisance to you and Malcolm, Frances. What about coming in with me, Lynne, and helping me pack? Then I'll drive down to Jane's, as I suppose I'm allowed to use the car now that the police have gone.'

'All right,' Lynne said. 'Is it far to Jane's? I'll go with you if you like.'

'No, let me get settled in first, but come and see me this evening,' Avril said. 'It isn't far beyond the Birds' house – a modern bungalow. And Frances and Malcolm, I do want to thank you for being so good to me. I don't know what I'd have done yesterday if you hadn't looked after me. Now I'll go in and pack a few things, then I'll come round for the dogs.'

'You didn't really mean what you said about having them put down, did you?' Malcolm said.

'Didn't I?' she said vaguely. 'I don't know, perhaps I didn't. Well, I'll be round presently to collect them.'

She opened the gate and she and Lynne went up the path to the house.

As we went on to ours, Malcolm said to Brian, 'What induced you to tell the yarn about Fred Dyer in Edgewater? Were you just enjoying shocking them all with a little gruesome gossip, or had you some end in view?'

'Not much of an end,' Brian said. 'But I really would like to know what brought him to Raneswood, and talking about it and seeing if there's any reaction is one of the ways of getting information. I could see the people at the next table listening, and that girl who waited on us lingered near us while I was talking, so I expect the story will be spread around fairly soon and something may come of it.'

'That seems rather hard on Fred,' I said. 'If he left Edgewater because he couldn't stand the atmosphere of suspicion there, he may soon have to be moving on from here.'

We had entered the house and could hear the barking of the dogs in the garden.

'That comes a bit hard on Sharon,' Malcolm said.

'Best thing that could happen to her,' Brian said. 'Even if he isn't the Edgewater murderer and didn't shoot Peter, I don't trust him. Anyway, if they really care for each other, she could go with him, though I think it would be a mistake.'

I thought of the frightened face that I had seen in the Green Man, and felt inclined to agree with Brian that the sooner Sharon parted from Fred Dyer, the better it would be for her. Yet I was quite convinced by then that he could not be the man whom I had seen at the Loxleys' gate.

Brian was going on, 'I wish Judy was here. She's so much shrewder than I am. I'd never have managed things as well at the school if it hadn't been for her, though she always kept herself in the background. She's got a way of seeing through people that is almost uncanny. I think, if you don't mind, I'll phone her now and tell her the latest developments.'

Malcolm and I left him in the hall with the telephone and went into the sitting room. I could not help thinking, as we settled down there, that our telephone bill for that quarter would be uncommonly large, but I was also thinking of something else which continued to tantalize me, as it had when we were at lunch. It was the look that I had seen on Avril's face when Brian had insisted that there was no difference between having her dogs put down and killing them. The look that had reminded me of something, though I had not been able to think of what. And suddenly I knew what it was, though as soon as I had thought of it, I dismissed it. I did not trust my own perception, for it was the look, exhausted, strained and ill, that I had seen a number of times on the faces of young women in the earliest stages of pregnancy.

CHAPTER 6

When Brian had finished his telephoning, he said that he would like to lie down and disappeared upstairs. Malcolm went upstairs to his autobiography. I stayed in a chair by the fire, so startled by the thought about Avril that had come into my mind that I felt wakeful and restless. For of course if there was anything in it, it probably altered everything that we had been thinking about Peter's murder. And then I fell asleep, which was the last thing that I had been expecting. Naturally, I only became aware that this had happened to me when I woke up. It puzzled me then that all of a sudden there was dusk in the room and I assumed for a moment that it was morning and that I must have woken unusually early. Then I noticed that I was fully dressed, that I was not in bed and that the electric fire was glowing in front of me. As I came gradually to my senses, I looked at my watch. It was nearly half-past five. It was too late for it to be worth getting tea and besides someone was ringing the front doorbell.

I went to answer it. Lynne was on the doorstep.

'Are you busy?' she asked. 'Am I a nuisance?'

I said that I was delighted to see her and led her into the sitting room. I turned on the lights and drew the curtains and offered her a drink, but she shook her head.

'No, thank you. I seem to have been drinking on and off all day,' she said. 'I just wanted to have a talk with you.'

'Do you want Malcolm too?' I asked. 'Shall I fetch him?'

I had noticed that the typewriter was silent. Then I

remembered that the divan in his room, on which Avril had slept the night before, had not been made up, and that the few things of hers that Brian and I had fetched from the house next door the night before had been forgotten and not taken to Jane's house with her other baggage.

'Oh, don't trouble him,' Lynne said, sitting down, 'I just wanted to tell you that I'm going back to London tomorrow. I don't seem able to be of any help here. In fact, all I do is bring the press down on you. If I hadn't come they wouldn't have bothered Avril nearly so much as they've been doing. I'm sorry about it, but I can't help it. I'm used to it and don't get much bothered by it, but she's finding it a horrible strain. They've pursued her out to Jane Kerwood's house and interviewed her and photographed her and nearly driven her mad. But that isn't what I meant to talk about. You're a close friend of Avril's, aren't you?'

Her face was pale and anxious and less beautiful than I had yet seen it. She was twisting her fingers together with nervous stress. She seemed to me to be in a state of wanting to talk and yet being half afraid of doing so.

'We're good friends, yes,' I said.

'Her closest friend here?'

'Perhaps I am. Yet I don't really know an awful lot about her.'

'Well, you remember what I told you about Peter this morning, don't you?'

'Yes.'

'Oh dear, I don't really know if I'm doing the right thing talking to you or not,' she said. 'Only I feel that someone here should know the truth about Avril, so that they can help her if she needs it. You see, she's pregnant.'

So my intuition about that had been right. It gave me no satisfaction.

'And of course,' she went on hurriedly, 'Peter couldn't have been the father. And she won't tell me who he was.

I suppose that's natural. I don't know if she means to have the child or have an abortion. I don't think she knows herself. And I don't know if there's any possibility that she'll marry the man, whoever he is. Tell me, do you know anything about a man called Hugh Maskell?'

'Did she tell you about him?' I asked.

'Yes, she said she thinks he wants to marry her, but she wouldn't say whether or not the child is his, or if it isn't, does he know about her being pregnant? And she said, anyway, even if she's right about him, she can't think of marriage now, it would be indecent. I suppose she's right. Yet if he really cares about her, he might be able to help her so much. What do you think? Is she right that he wants to marry her?'

'Quite right, I think, to go by what he told me this morning,' I answered.

'What sort of man is he?'

'Well, he's in his sixties, which might be a bit old for Avril. He was a surgeon of some distinction, I believe, but he retired early because his wife, Anna, was dying of leukaemia and he stayed at home to care for her. She died about two years ago. And it's a generally accepted thing in the village that he'll marry again, and there was always gossip about him and Avril. She was a close friend of Anna's, you see, and used to spend a lot of time in the house with her, but naturally people didn't talk of marriage, as Avril already had a husband. But now that Peter's dead – well, I don't know.'

'But you like him? You think he'd be good to her? You see, I'm thinking that once the case of Peter's death is solved, I might take her out to Hollywood with me. But I wouldn't want to interfere if there's the chance of her making a good marriage.'

I wondered what her ideas of a good marriage were. She had tried it three times, I believed, without success.

'I'm sure he'd be good to her after his fashion,' I said,

111

'but whether or not that would be Avril's fashion, I don't know.'

'You realize, of course, that unless she has an abortion, she isn't going to be able to keep her pregnancy secret for very long, and that may alter the way people think of Peter's murder. Someone, and it might be Hugh Maskell, had a motive for killing Peter.'

'Won't it be assumed that the child was Peter's?'

'But I told you . . . Oh!' She clapped a hand over her mouth. 'Of course, they don't know anything about that, do they, and they won't unless you tell them. Are you going to tell the police about it? Do you think they ought to know?'

'I think we'd better wait and see. If it turns out that it had nothing whatever to do with the murder, I don't see why we need to enlighten them.'

'I'm so glad that's what you feel. You see, if I'd known anything about Avril having a child, I'd never have told you about Peter's trouble. I only told you, as I'm telling you all this now, because I thought you seemed the kind of person who would help her if she needed it. But I'm sure it will be far the best for her if people assume the child was Peter's.'

I thought that she was undoubtedly right, though I had hardly begun to take in what this new knowledge did to the case.

'Of course, now I realize why she wants to get rid of the dogs,' she went on. 'She'll want to get away from here, whether it's to London or somewhere else, and travelling with three big dogs wouldn't be exactly easy. I wonder what she'll do. And I wonder if it has anything to do with Peter's murder. I can't believe it somehow. It's so easy to deal with that kind of thing nowadays.'

'I'm wondering if Peter himself knew about the pregnancy.'

'What do you think he'd have done if he did?'

It was a question that made me realize how little I knew

the Loxleys. I had thought of them for some time as friends, but the truth was that I knew next to nothing about the emotional side of their natures. I had a moderate understanding of Avril, but Peter I knew hardly at all. Though I had had the feeling for some time that their marriage was not a happy one, I could not have said what seemed to me to be wrong with it, or indeed why I had the feeling. I had a vague sort of idea that the basis of the trouble was their lack of children, that Avril's compensation for this with her dogs was really a considerable annoyance to Peter, and that possibly he compensated for this in ways of his own, for which the flat in Fulham came in useful. But I had not the least evidence for this.

'I suspect it might have depended to some extent on who the father of the child was,' I said.

She looked puzzled. 'Why should that make a difference?'

'Don't you think it would be harder for him to tolerate it, and bring up the child as his own, if the man in question was a friend of his, whom he might have to go on seeing day after day?'

'You're thinking about Hugh Maskell.'

'There are other possibilities besides Hugh.'

'You think it would really be easier for him to take if it was just a bit of random promiscuity?'

'Don't you think so yourself?'

She was giving me a steady, interested stare as if what I had said surprised her.

'I suppose I do,' she said at length. 'It might feel more like simply having an adopted child. All the same, I think he'd have insisted on an abortion or a divorce. But if Avril didn't want the divorce she could bring out Peter's limitation in her defence, and that would be rather humiliating for him.'

'Did she speak to you at all about the divorce she might have had?'

'No. When I raised the question she simply brushed it

113

aside, saying that in any case it didn't arise now, which of course is true. In a way it was a bit queer, the one thing she seemed to want to talk about was money. She said she was going to see their solicitor in the next day or two, to find out if he would advance her money before the whole financial situation was cleared up. I said I was sure he would, but that if she was in any difficulty I'd gladly lend her anything she wanted. Then she took my breath away. She said she wanted ten thousand pounds and she wanted it soon. I promised her I'd let her have it, but it's rather extraordinary, isn't it?'

'It has an unwholesome smell of blackmail to me,' I said.

'Blackmail,' she said thoughtfully, still with that intent look fixed on my face, searching and curious. 'What could anyone blackmail her for? She can't have had anything to do with Peter's murder. She was in London with me.'

'Suppose she had an accomplice, who now wants to be paid off.'

'The man in the red wig?'

'It isn't impossible, is it?'

'In that case, it wouldn't have been Hugh Maskell, would it?'

'No. I can imagine Hugh committing murder for passion, but not for money.'

'But you aren't serious about this, are you? Why commit a murder when divorce is so easy? I don't think that ten thousand pounds was blackmail. I think it was because she's all in a hurry to set up a new life for herself, and actually, at the moment she isn't capable of thinking about anything clearly. And ten thousand pounds won't go so very far these days. If she wants to make the flat in London suitable for a child, and if she wants to have it privately, not on the NHS, which is quite likely, it'll soon dwindle away. No, I think you can put the thought of blackmail out of your mind. Now, I'd better be going.'

At that moment the doorbell rang.

I went to answer it, and found Fred Dyer on the door-step.

He was about the last person I was expecting, and I suppose I showed it. He looked irritated.

'If this is inconvenient for you, I can come some other time,' he said abruptly, 'but there are some things I'd like to talk over with you.'

'No, it's all right. Come in,' I said and took him into the sitting room.

Lynne had stood up and looked as if she was just preparing to take her leave. I introduced them to one another. She looked at Fred with her searching, inquisitive stare. He looked at her with his usual appearance of studying something much further away than she was.

'I didn't think of your having a guest,' he said. 'As I said, I can go away and come back some other time.'

'I'm just leaving,' Lynne said. 'Don't worry about me.'

'Going to the Green Man?' he asked.

'Yes.'

But she did not leave. She sat down on the arm of a chair and gave Fred one of her most charming smiles.

She murmured, '"Oh, Romeo, Romeo, wherefore art thou Romeo?"'

He smiled back; his not unfriendly but impersonal smile.

'That's what I've been asking myself in recent times,' he said. 'Of course, I wouldn't have been if Juliet had been anyone but Sharon.'

'She persuaded you to take the part?' Lynne said.

'Yes, and it was just because of her own shyness. She's dead scared of most of the people here.'

'Ah,' she said, 'I thought she was scared of something.'

It surprised me that Lynne had had the same impression of the girl as I had had.

'But now, of course, it isn't going to happen,' he said. 'The show. And that's a relief to me. I'm no sort of an actor.'

'I wonder if that's true,' Lynne said. 'I wonder very

much. Anyway, I think it's a mistake to have cancelled the thing. Going on with it, if not quite immediately, might have helped the community here to get back to normal.'

'They'll do that anyway, as soon as the press move on to other things,' he said. 'As long as they're around it keeps up the excitement. And that's partly your fault, I believe, Mrs Denison. Murder with a film star thrown in is a good deal more exhilarating than murder pure and simple.'

She gave a little shrug of her shoulders. 'You may be right, but the film star is going back to London tomorrow. I don't like to hear murder called exhilarating. That's going a little far for me.'

'Well, don't we hear about it on television nearly every night?' he said. 'We're a pretty blood-soaked generation. I suppose it doesn't quite keep up with what it would be in wartime, but we do our best.'

'I don't think I like you,' she said, but she had still a faint smile on her face. 'Even if you aren't the man whom Mrs Chance saw at the gate next door, I don't think I'd ever trust you very far.'

'I've been used to that for some time,' he answered. 'I've come to expect it. But they haven't lost much time, have they, in telling the story of my murky past.'

'You mean what happened in Edgewater?'

'Yes.'

'Well, I've been told you were suspected of three murders, without there being any real evidence against you, and that you came here to get away from the atmosphere of suspicion. But that doesn't seem to have worked, does it? Suspicion has reared its ugly head again.'

'Yes, it's definitely a mistake to have red hair. In the next place I move on to, I'll get a dye job done. What d'you recommend? Black hair or a bleach?'

I had noticed that while they were talking, Fred's local accent had entirely disappeared. A public school and

Oxford or Cambridge seemed to be the most probable background for him.

'But *are* you thinking of moving on, Fred?' I asked.

'Well, wouldn't you, if you were me?' he said.

'And will Sharon go with you?'

'I don't know. You'll have to ask her.'

'Of course you do know, and you don't mean to take her with you,' Lynne said. She stood up. 'Anyway, I must be going. I suppose you came here to talk to Mrs or Mr Chance and I've been getting in your way. I hope that *Romeo and Juliet* goes ahead and that you stick to your part, Mr Dyer. I think you might make a success of it. Goodbye for now, Frances. Perhaps we'll meet again before I leave for London.'

I saw her to the door.

When she had gone, I returned to the sitting room and found Fred still standing where I had left him. He gave me a grin.

'I didn't make much of a hit there, did I?' he said.

'As a matter of fact, I thought you did,' I answered. 'It's just her way of putting things. Would you like a drink?'

'Now, that would be really nice,' he said.

'Sherry or whisky?'

'Whisky, please.'

I went to the cupboard and got out whisky for him and sherry for myself. As I did so, I listened to the sound of Malcolm's typewriter. I could hear it ticking away quite rapidly, so I gave up the thought that I had had a moment before that I would fetch him down to hear what Fred had to say. Malcolm was always irritable if he was interrupted when the work was going nicely.

'I suppose I might have offered to take her down to the pub in my van,' Fred said, 'but it seemed to me it would be tactless. She might not like driving alone through the dark with someone who may have committed a number of sex murders. And after all, Edgewater may not have

117

been the beginning of it. I may have been getting away with it for years.'

I gave him his drink.

'Well, sit down, Fred,' I said, 'and tell me why you came to see me.'

We both sat down, and Fred contemplated the drink he held for a little while, before he started to speak. When he did, it was an abrupt question.

'Mrs Chance, do you believe I shot Mr Loxley?'

I met his look which seemed so direct, yet was in fact so evasive.

'Suppose I do, Fred,' I said, 'I've told the police what I saw, or thought I saw, so things are up to them now, aren't they? What I believe isn't really important.'

'What you thought you saw,' he said. 'You've some doubts about it, haven't you? You aren't sure it was me whom you saw at the gate.'

'No, I'm inclined to think it wasn't. I think whoever it was, was wearing a wig, and it seems strange for a red-haired man to choose a red wig if he wants to disguise himself. And he was wearing gloves, which I've never seen you do. And he'd walked up to the house instead of coming in your van, as you usually do. And he arrived just at the time which you'd know was the time when Mrs Henderson would be leaving the house. You'd have known you'd only got to be ten minutes later and she wouldn't be there to identify you. That I came along just then was something that you couldn't have expected, but it isn't really important. It's what Mrs Henderson saw that counts. And she was very struck, as I was, with your uncharacteristic behaviour, keeping turned away from her so that she never saw your face. Well, does it sound as if I believe you shot Mr Loxley?'

He sipped his whisky.

'Thank you,' he said. 'You've put it very plainly and you've taken a great load off my mind. Have you yourself ever had the experience of being suspected of horrible things that you haven't done?'

'No, I don't think I have.'

'You should try it some time. It does peculiar things to you.'

'You're thinking of the Edgewater crimes.'

'Of more than that. No, that isn't quite what I mean. But the feeling that the suspicion that hunted you down is never going to let go of you turns you into someone who doesn't seem like yourself. You start seeing yourself with other people's eyes. Have you ever asked yourself, Mrs Chance, where I came from before I came to Raneswood?'

'Actually, I never thought much about it,' I said, 'until Mr Hewlett told us you'd come from Edgewater, and what happened to you there.'

'And before Edgewater? And haven't you ever asked yourself what a man like me is doing, earning his living by doing odd jobs around a village?'

'Suppose I take the second question first. Yes, I've wondered about that, but perhaps I've thought less about you than you think. Villages have a way of harbouring oddities. One rather takes them for granted. And there's been a rumour around, as I expect you know, that you're a poet, and if it's true, then doing odd jobs while you write away seems a sensible way of keeping going.'

'A poet – good God!' he said, and gave a harsh little laugh. 'And you believed it?'

'I really didn't think about it much, Fred,' I said.

'Yes, I see what you mean. It's just that I've been altogether too egotistic. I've thought people were wondering about me when actually they weren't bothered about me at all. Well, let me tell you, I've never written a line of poetry in my life. So that's cleared up. Now to go back to my other question. What was I doing before I came to Edgewater? You'll tell me, I suppose, that you never thought about that either.'

'I don't think I ever did. I think, once Mr Hewlett told us he'd known you there, I just assumed you belonged there. Probably had been born and bred there. But that isn't so?'

'It certainly isn't.'

I could see that it irked him that so little thought had been given to him, that it had taken a crime in which he might or might not be involved, to make him to some extent a centre of attraction. His pride was hurt when he found that we had not all been thinking a great deal of him.

'Then where *did* you come from?' I asked in as interested a tone as I could, wanting to placate him. I did not like the feeling that there was anger in him only just below the surface.

'London,' he answered. 'But I didn't go straight from there to Edgewater. There was a certain interval of a few years; not the happiest few years in my not very successful life, but perhaps the most influential. They've cast their shadow over everything I've tried to do since.'

'Are you telling me that they were spent in prison?'

'That's right.'

'For what?'

'Oh, not for strangling girls and tying black plastic bags over their heads. But still, I've got blood on my hands. I deserved what I got.'

'Go on,' I said. 'Tell me what you did. That's what you want, isn't it? You want to tell me what you did.'

He made a small gesture with his hands as if he were offering me all that they held.

'One has to talk sometimes,' he said. 'It might as well be to you as to anyone. You've got a good deal of power over me at the moment, so you might as well know the worst. I and a friend had a habit of pinching cars and going joy-riding. On the whole, it wasn't very serious. When we were tired of it we'd leave the car somewhere and get home by bus, and the owner would probably get

120

it back next day. But one day things went wrong. I'll never forget it. We were going along much too fast and overtook one of those damned great lorries and couldn't see what was ahead of it till we'd almost passed it, and what was there was a crossroads with a gang of children waiting to cross the road until the thing had gone by, and another car was coming towards us. To avoid being smashed by it, we swung in to the left, trying to get ahead of the lorry, and didn't see some lights had just changed, and it had just stopped, and the kids were starting to stream across the road. We went slam into them, killed one and injured several more. It was manslaughter and we both went to prison.'

'Were you driving?' I asked.

'Yes, but that didn't make much difference. If my friend had been driving, he'd have done the same sooner or later. They gave him a year less than me, but that was all. Well, I did my time and was out and then my real troubles began. Because who was going to give a job to someone with a record like mine? If it hadn't been children it might not have been so bad, but as soon as it came out what I'd done, there was no job, thank you, it had already been filled. So naturally, I changed my name. I did it more than once. But you don't stand much of a chance of getting a job if you've no references. So I decided to go down a bit in the world, get rid of my classy accent, and take anything that was going, from window-cleaning to washing cars and gardening. It worked surprisingly well. If you don't care how small a job is, there are plenty going, and you get paid in cash, so there are no worries about income tax. I've always been a pretty good mechanic and I'd get a reputation in a district as a useful sort of character to know. Then I drifted into a job in a garage in Edgewater and stayed there for some time. I liked it. I liked the feeling of stability it gave me for a change. I picked up with a nice girl and though I didn't intend to stay there for long, I believe I could have stayed for quite a time. And then that bloody business about those three murdered girls blew up, and for no reason at all, I got suspected.'

'But that had nothing to do with your killing a child and injuring several more and doing your time in prison.'

'Nothing whatever. It was just a piece of foul bad luck. A woman, as it might be yourself, saw someone with red hair leaving the scene of the crime and swore it was me. My girlfriend gave me an alibi, but that didn't cut much ice, and later the woman changed her mind. She saw me in an identification parade and said it might have been anyone in it whom she'd seen. So I got off, I wasn't arrested, but I wasn't by any means thought to be innocent. That's when I really began to discover how suspicion can ruin your life. I stood it for a time, then I told my boss I was leaving, and I told the police too and told them I was going to look for work in Otterswell. But I wasn't lucky there and I was thinking of moving on when I met Sharon. We met in a pub where she'd gone for a drink with some friends, and somehow we got talking and she said she thought I'd stand a much better chance of getting odd jobs if I went to a village where there wasn't even a garage, for instance Raneswood. So that's how I got here. And again, when I'm doing nicely, and have quite a nice bit of cash in the bank, and thinking life quite pleasant, a murder's committed and I'm the man on the spot who must have done it . . . Yes, what did you say?'

I had only begun to say something, then stopped. I thought for a moment, then said, 'Does Sharon know all this story?'

'Most of it,' he answered.

'Which are the bits she doesn't know? The girls in Edgewater, or the manslaughter?'

'Oh, she knows all about them both. What she doesn't know is that I was once on the edge of going to a university; also that I've got quite a bit of money stashed away. When I've got a bit more I'll be moving on. She does know that. She knows what we've got isn't for keeps, and she's accepted it.'

'When you move on, where are you planning to go?'

'Australia,' he answered promptly.

'I don't believe they'll let you in if you have a criminal record.'

'Well, there are other places.'

'Where you think you'll be able to start a really new life.'

'Mrs Chance, it wouldn't surprise me if within a month of my getting there a murder's committed by a man with red hair and someone positively identifies me. Meanwhile . . .'

'Yes?'

'Did you mean what you said about having seen someone at the Loxleys' gate who wasn't me?'

Just then the telephone began to ring, so I did not have to answer him. I went to the telephone and found the caller was Judy Hewlett, ringing up from Cheshire. We chatted for a minute or two, each of us asking how the other was, and saying that murder was very unsettling, then Judy asked if she could speak to Brian and I went upstairs to summon him.

When he came down and started to talk to Judy, Fred, overhearing some of it observed, 'That's Mrs Hewlett, isn't it? I always liked her. She's really got brains. She always believed in my innocence.'

'Perhaps it would help you if she were here now,' I said.

'I wish she were. But you haven't answered my question, Mrs Chance.'

So after all I had to answer it.

'Yes, I meant it,' I said.

'That it was someone disguised as me, probably wearing that red wig that's kept with all the theatrical gear in the village hall?'

'That does seem likely.'

'Thank you. You've taken a big weight off my mind.'

'But I could be wrong.'

'Ah, don't spoil it. Stick to what you think.'

He finished his whisky and stood up as if he were about to leave, but just then Malcolm came down the stairs and into the room.

He looked surprised to see Fred, and Fred remained where he was, instead of leaving as he had intended.

'I've been having a very interesting talk with Mrs Chance,' he said. 'You should get her to tell you all the things we've discussed.'

'I found it interesting,' I said, 'but I wouldn't have called it exactly a discussion. Fred's been telling me a lot about himself, Malcolm. I did little more than listen.'

'Then have another drink, Fred, and let me hear from you what you've been telling my wife. I'd sooner hear it from you than second-hand from her.'

Fred gave one of his remote smiles, sat down again and accepted the drink that Malcolm poured out for him. In the hall, Brian was still talking to Judy. By now, I thought, she must know as much about the murder as we did. I was glad that the call had come from her and that it would go on the Cheshire bill, not on ours.

'Where d'you think I should begin, Mrs Chance?' Fred asked.

'I should say with that joy-ride of yours,' I said.

'I was afraid you'd say that. Oddly enough, you may think, it isn't one of the things I enjoy talking about. In fact, I don't believe I've talked about it to anyone for several years.'

'I thought you said you'd told Sharon all about it.'

'Did I? Well yes, I think I did tell her about it. But that hardly counts.'

'Why not?' I asked.

'Well, talking to your girlfriend can sometimes feel like talking to yourself. And she doesn't ask questions, she just listens. Mr Chance, is it true that they've dropped the idea of doing *Romeo and Juliet*?'

'I believe so,' Malcolm said, 'and not a bad thing, in my opinion. It was much too ambitious for them. They'd have done better with Noël Coward or some Lonsdale.'

'I was going to say, if they're going on with it,' Fred said, 'that they'd better find themselves another Romeo. I don't think I'll be here much longer.'

'Do you mean to say that you're expecting to be arrested?' Malcolm asked, with raised eyebrows.

'What he means is that he's taking off for Australia, or some remote place, as soon as he can afford it,' I said.

'And Mr Bird would make a much better Romeo than me,' Fred said.

'We'd still have to find a Mercutio,' Malcolm said, which was more macabre than was characteristic of him. 'Now, what's this about a joy-ride?'

'Shall we wait until Mr Hewlett comes in?' Fred suggested. 'He'd also want the story from the horse's mouth, I expect.'

His reluctance to start made me wonder for the first time since he and I had been talking together how much of what he had told me was the truth. Not that I could see what he might have to gain by inventing a story about killing a child and going to prison. But perhaps it was the later part of his history that he did not want to repeat. For instance, what had brought him to Raneswood. Had it really been chance, as he had said, or had he had some motive in coming?

At last we heard the tinkle of the telephone as Brian put it down, then he came into the room.

'Hello, Jack, I didn't know you were here,' he said.

'Fred – or Jack – is about to tell us something about his past,' Malcolm said. 'Frances has heard it already and seems to have found it interesting. But I want a drink and I expect you do too. Then we can settle down comfortably to listen.'

He went to the drinks cupboard and poured out sherry for Brian and whisky for himself, which was not his usual drink, except in times of crisis. It made me wonder what his real feelings were about Fred. Was he acutely repelled by him? Did he think we were entertaining a murderer?

Sitting down, he said, 'Now what about this joy-ride?'

'I think I'll begin a little earlier than that,' Fred said, 'because I expect you've been a bit puzzled since we got to know each other about my background. Well, my father was a solicitor, a partner in a firm with offices in Bedford Square —'

He was interrupted by the telephone ringing again.

'You'd better answer that,' Malcolm said to me. 'It's nearly always for you.'

I went out to the hall, picked up the telephone and said, 'Frances Chance speaking.'

'Frances!' said a breathless voice which I recognized as Jane Kerwood's. 'It's fearful! It's — oh, I don't know how to tell you, I'll just have to blurt it straight out. Lynne Denison's dead. She's been killed. Strangled. And she's got a black plastic bag over her head. She's in the alley beside the Green Man. We've called the police, but they haven't got here yet ... Oh, there they are, thank heavens! I'll ring you again later when we know a little more. Goodbye now.'

She rang off.

As she did so, I heard in the distance the police sirens. At the same time, as I put our telephone down and stood for a moment with my hand on it, staring blindly at nothing, I was thinking that Fred Dyer had an alibi that nothing could disprove.

CHAPTER 7

I told them what I had heard on the telephone.

Fred Dyer did not wait for a moment. He was across the hall in a few strides and out through the front door, slamming it shut behind him. A moment later, I heard his van start up.

'What do we do?' I asked Malcolm.

'Nothing,' he answered. 'If the police want us, they'll come for us.'

'I think I'm going to go down there,' Brian said. 'I want to know what's happened.'

'It looks, at any rate,' I said, 'as if your suspicions of Fred were without foundation.'

'It does,' he said. 'It makes me feel rather ashamed. He's had a lot of trouble for nothing.'

'I wonder if it was really for nothing,' Malcolm said. 'It may look as if the Edgewater murderer is at home in Raneswood, but did Fred Dyer know that, or was it really chance that brought him here?'

'Well, I'm going down there to find out what's happened,' Brian said. 'You don't want to come with me?'

Malcolm shook his head. Brian did not ask me if I wanted to go with him, as if he took it for granted that the scene of a murder was not suitable for a woman. I was quite ready to agree with him. I sat down again with my drink and Malcolm sat down with his, and we waited in silence. I was not sure what we were waiting for, whether it was for Brian to come back with information about Lynne Denison's death, or for the police to visit us,

127

or for the telephone to ring yet again. It felt as if something must happen, though why it should happen to us, I could not have said.

At last, after what felt like a long time, Malcolm said, 'What's for supper?'

'Omelettes, I think,' I said. 'I haven't cooked anything.'

'We'll have to wait for Brian.'

'Yes, I don't see why he had to rush off like that.'

'I suppose he has a feeling of intimacy with this kind of crime.'

'Will he be able to tell the police anything useful, d'you think?'

'He can tell them Fred isn't the murderer here, so probably wasn't in Edgewater either.'

'I suppose that does follow.'

'It seems probable.'

'I've got some mushrooms. Shall I make mushroom omelettes?'

'Sounds good.'

'But if Brian doesn't come back fairly soon I shall probably be too drunk to make them. I'm afraid all I want to do at the moment is have another drink.'

Malcolm got up to supply me with one. Bringing it to me, he asked, 'What were you and Fred talking about all this afternoon? He'd only just begun to tell us when the telephone rang.'

I told him the story of Fred's past life that he had told me. Malcolm's face was impassive as he listened. As I finished, he got up and poured out another drink for himself, then relapsed into another silence.

After a while, he muttered, 'Blood on his hands . . . He used that phrase, did he, that he'd got blood on his hands?'

'Yes,' I said.

'Did he seem remorseful, or indifferent, or what?'

'Fairly indifferent, I thought, but he's had to live with the fact for a long time. He probably gave up beating his chest about it a long time ago.'

Malcolm leant back in his chair, gazing thoughtfully into his whisky.

'I wonder if having once killed an individual makes it easier or harder to kill the next one,' he said.

'But the one thing we can be sure of is that he hasn't killed anybody.'

'You're still sure he wasn't the man at the Loxleys' gate?'

'That man was in disguise, I'm sure of that.'

'And he may or may not be the man who's murdered Lynne. Her murder and Peter's are so different that I find it easiest to believe they were done by different people, for reasons that may have no connection.'

'Yes, I suppose that's what I think too.'

Again we fell silent. It was about an hour before Brian returned. He came in then with dragging footsteps, as if he were very tired, and with his sharp-featured face looking drawn and curiously bitter. He dropped into a chair.

'They've got him,' he said.

'Fred?' Malcolm said in surprise.

'No, no, Kevin Bird.'

'*Kevin?*' Malcolm said incredulously. 'They've arrested Kevin?'

'Yes, and he's spilling his guts, telling them everything he's done. Now for pity's sake, get me a drink, Malcolm, and give me a few minutes to get my thoughts in order.'

Malcolm gave him a whisky, then returned to the chair where he had been sitting, and waited.

Brian was panting slightly, either because of the speed at which he had come up the lane, or because of a sense of excitement that he could not control. At last, he drew a deep breath and seemed to relax, though there was still a look of shock on his face.

'Yes,' he said. 'Well, that's what's happened. She was found only a few minutes after she'd been killed. Her body was in that alley between the Green Man and the Birds' house. And as you'll remember, there's a high brick wall

129

enclosing the Birds' garden and there's a gate in it, and the alley leads through to the car park behind the pub. A young couple had just left their car in the park and were walking towards the entrance to the alley when they saw the gate open and something dumped out of it. And that was Lynne. She had a black plastic sack over her head and some flex round her throat, and she was quite warm and at first they didn't believe she was dead. They tore the sack off and one of them rushed into the pub to phone for a doctor, but of course a lot of people who were in the pub streamed out to see what had happened, and someone phoned for the police. Your friend Jane Kerwood was there with Hugh Maskell and she took it into her head to phone you. I asked her why she did that and she said it was because you were a friend of Lucille Bird's and would want to help her. By then the people from the pub had got Kevin cornered in his house and handed him over like a present when the police arrived. And he broke down completely. Started to cry and scream and went on to confessing everything. Not just the killing of poor Lynne, but those other women in Edgewater too, besides two or three others we haven't heard about. It was a hideous sight, a human being coming apart at the seams and sheer evil pouring out through all the gaps.'

'Where was Lucille while this was happening?' I asked.

'Out playing bridge somewhere,' Brian said. 'I didn't wait for them to find her. I suppose she knows by now what's happened.'

'But did she know that Kevin was the Edgewater murderer?' I demanded. 'Has she kept quiet about it all this time?'

'I'm sure she hasn't,' Malcolm said. 'It may be partly her fault that he's turned into the kind of thing he is, but she can't have known what he'd done. I won't believe that.'

'But how could Kevin get away to Edgewater as often as he must have without her knowing?'

Malcolm spoke to Brian. 'Those murders were about a year ago, weren't they?'

'Yes,' Brian said.

'And about a year ago Lucille was in Canada and Kevin had no one to keep an eye on him. That's easily enough explained. But what took Lynne out to the Birds' house this evening if Lucille wasn't there?'

'I gathered that she had a telephone call almost as soon as she got back to the pub and she went out again very soon afterwards. The idea about that seems to be that the call was from Kevin, asking her round for a drink without mentioning that his mother wouldn't be there, and it isn't known yet how long he kept her there before killing her. The doctor had only just arrived, and I don't suppose he can tell much. It'll be up to the forensic people to tie up the loose ends. But it seems she'd had a blow on her head before she was strangled. Of course, dumping her like that in the alley was an act of lunacy, which makes one feel that Kevin had really lost all grip on himself. He may even have wanted to be arrested and confess all his crimes. He may not have been able to carry the load of guilt any longer, or perhaps it was a kind of vanity. Don't mass murderers sometimes want to have their great achievements recognized?'

'I remember when we were in the Green Man at lunch time, Kevin couldn't keep his eyes off Lynne,' I said. 'I suppose he'd got her selected already as his next victim.'

'But why should he murder Peter?' Malcolm said. 'That doesn't fit, does it?'

'There's a possible motive for it now,' Brian said. 'If Loxley had somehow found out the truth about Kevin, then it would be worth Kevin's while to get rid of him. And he'd have known where he could lay his hands on a red wig. Frances, could the man you saw at the Loxleys' gate have been Kevin in a red wig?'

I nodded. 'It could have been. But it could have been

several other people. I'm not going to try to identify anybody any more.'

'Anyway, how could he have got hold of Peter's gun?' Malcolm asked. 'Or do you think it was Peter who brought out the gun when he realized Kevin was going to attack him, and Kevin managed to wrench it away from him and shot him more or less accidentally? It makes one wonder . . .'

'Yes?' Brian said as Malcolm hesitated.

'It makes one wonder if Peter could have been black-mailing Kevin,' Malcolm said. 'If he'd somehow found out the truth about him . . . But no, Peter was as rich as Kevin. He'd no need to get money out of him. But he might simply have been threatening to hand on what he knew to the police. That's more likely.'

'But how could he have found out the truth about Kevin?' I asked.

'Finding that out is a job for the police, fortunately,' Malcolm answered.

'And they may never find out the truth,' Brian said, 'unless Kevin, in his present mood, pours it all out to them. That's quite possible. On the other hand, he may withdraw everything he's said once his mother's in charge and she's found him a lawyer. At the least, he ought to get away with a plea of diminished responsibility.'

'I suppose there's no question that what he's saying about having murdered Lynne is true,' I said. 'Did that young couple who found her actually see Kevin at the gate in the wall?'

'I'm not sure, but I don't think there's any question that what he's said himself is true,' Brian answered. 'He's determined now to be convicted.'

I finished my drink and went out to the kitchen to make the omelettes for supper, but I did not think much of what I was doing and they were not very successful. But it did not matter as no one had any appetite. That a woman who had been talking to us in the afternoon should in the little time since then have been atrociously killed made the meal seem singularly unimportant. Yet habit made it seem essential to provide it. The ordinary routine of the day had to be maintained. Whether I should have felt that so strongly if I had been younger, I did not know. Probably not, I thought. But as things were, routine seemed something to cling to. After the omelettes, we had coffee, set the dishwasher going and settled down once more in the sitting room. It was only a little while after that that Inspector Holroyd arrived.

He and the usual sergeant sat down in the sitting room, gratefully accepted drinks and agreed with one another that it felt good to take the weight off their feet.

Then the inspector said, 'I imagine you know why we've come. There's some information we believe you can give us.'

'About Lynne Denison?' Malcolm said.

'Yes, for one thing,' the inspector agreed. 'And about Fred Dyer, too. We believe they were both here in the late afternoon.'

'That's right,' Malcolm said. 'You must ask my wife about them. Most of the time they were here, I was upstairs working, and Mr Hewlett, I believe, was in his room, sound asleep. Is that right, Brian?'

'Absolutely,' Brian said. 'But how did you know they'd been here, Inspector?'

'Dyer's girlfriend, Sharon Sawyer, told us,' the inspector answered. 'Her story is that Dyer came in, said, "That's one murder they can't suspect me of," gave her a rough outline of how he'd met Lynne Denison here and had stayed until after you got the news of the murder, then packed a bag, got in his van and drove away. He didn't tell her where he was thinking of going, but the van's gone all right and there's no sign of him.'

'But why should he choose to vanish just when there really can't be any suspicion of him?' I said. 'It sounds very strange.'

'Perhaps not as strange as all that,' Inspector Holroyd said. 'As I think Mr Hewlett found out when he was down at the Green Man a little while ago, Kevin Bird has confessed to the murder of Mrs Denison, as well as to the three in Edgewater. In fact, there was no stopping him confessing. And along with it all, he claims to have been paying blackmail to Dyer, and if that's true, it's pretty serious for Dyer. Not only is blackmail itself a serious offence, but when it's related to the covering up of several murders it looks very black indeed. But before we go into that, I'd like to check on the truth of Dyer's alibi for Mrs Denison's murder. Was he here with you, Mrs Chance, at the significant time?'

'Oh yes, there's no doubt of that,' I said. 'First Mrs Denison came and when she'd been here a little while, Fred Dyer turned up, and they talked to each other for a short time about nothing in particular, then she left, and I remember he said that it wouldn't have been very tactful of him to offer to see her down to the pub, as he was suspected of murdering several women, and he stayed on until we had a telephone call from Miss Kerwood, telling us that Mrs Denison had been killed, at which he left in rather a hurry. It seemed a bit odd, the way he took off, particularly as I remember saying to myself that this time there was no question that he had an alibi, but what you've just told us about the blackmail explains that.'

'Why did he come to see you?' the inspector asked. 'Did he explain that?'

'I think it was mostly to make sure that I was going to stick to it that the man I saw at the Loxleys' gate wasn't him, but someone in disguise. But he told me a good deal about himself as well. He told me how he'd killed a child, joy-riding, and had gone to prison for it, and how he hadn't been able to get a job when he came out, and had taken to odd jobs as the only way to keep going. I think he just drifted into Edgewater by chance, and there he did manage to get a job in a garage. He left it, he said, because he couldn't stand the atmosphere of suspicion that had developed around him after he'd been identified by a woman there as a murderer. But he also claimed to have arrived in Raneswood by chance, and now we know better about that, don't we?'

'Yes, it seems probable that having discovered who the real murderer was, he followed him here,' the inspector said, 'and has been milking him ever since. We don't know yet how he discovered Bird was the killer – a pathological killer if there ever was one – but it was probably just a chance that he saw one of the crimes being committed.'

'Inspector, has Bird confessed to the killing of Peter Loxley?' Brian asked.

'No, and he gets very indignant when he's questioned about it,' the inspector said. 'He seems to take it as a kind of insult. It's not *his* kind of murder, that's what he seems to be saying.'

'And you're no further on with that?' Malcolm said.

'No, though we've been finding out a thing or two about Loxley. Did you know that he was once engaged to Miss Kerwood? It was only after he married Avril Loxley that Miss Kerwood took off on her travels and writing her book. That might give her a motive for wanting Loxley killed, but whatever disguise the man whom Mrs Chance saw was wearing, I think you're quite certain he couldn't have been a woman, aren't you, Mrs Chance?'

'Absolutely,' I said. 'He was much too tall and muscular.'

But here was the explanation of Jane's broken heart, I thought, and was ashamed to find myself wondering if she could have persuaded some tall and muscular man to take her revenge for her.

When the police left, I said that I was going to call in on Lucille. We had never been close friends, but the thought of what she must be suffering now was not one that could easily be put aside. She had other friends, and it seemed

135

certain that they would be taking care of her, but simply to say that and find it an adequate excuse for doing nothing myself did not agree with how I was feeling. Malcolm said that he would come with me and he was just about to set out to get the Rover out of the garage when the doorbell rang.

This time it was Sharon Sawyer.

She stood on the doorstep, looking at me speechlessly, as if she expected me to tell her why she was there. She looked so pretty and so forlorn that I unthinkingly put an arm round her to draw her inside. She was as stiff in my embrace as if she were made of wood. I dropped my arm, but I took one of her hands. It was tense and stiff and very cold.

'What is it, Sharon?' I asked.

'He's gone,' she said.

'Fred?'

'Yes.'

'He's left you?'

'Yes.'

That did not quite explain why she had come to us, but it was enough to make me delay my visit to Lucille. I drew her into the sitting room. Malcolm offered her a drink, but she shook her head. I offered her coffee, but she muttered, 'No, thank you – nothing. I just want to ask you something. I don't want to be a nuisance.'

'It wouldn't be any nuisance,' I said, but she shook her head again and even seemed doubtful if she ought to sit down.

We persuaded her to do that, however, and to take off the anorak that she was wearing; an action that seemed to help her to overcome her extreme shyness, or whatever it was that made her so frightened of us. She leant back in the chair, crossing one foot over the other and locking her hands together and looking from one to the other of us again as if she expected us to explain her presence. She had the scared look in her eyes that I had seen there at lunch in the Green Man.

Suddenly I wondered if someone had advised her to come to us, and she really did not know why. But who would have done that?

'Sharon, did Fred tell you to come to us?' I asked.

She nodded, but did not answer.

'Why?' I said.

At last she said, 'He told me you could give him an alibi and I needn't be afraid there'd be anything phoney about it.' Her voice was so low that it was almost inaudible. 'I gave him a phoney alibi, you see. He said if I didn't, he'd kill me. Of course, he didn't mean it, he just meant he'd do something horrible to me, and he'd got me so scared of him by then I couldn't think. I often got like that with him. I don't know why I loved him when he frightened me so. He used to frighten me in all sorts of ways. He'd hurt me just a little and make me think he was going to do more. For instance, he'd take hold of one of my hands and bend the fingers backwards till I almost screamed with the pain, and he'd tell me he could easily break the lot if he felt like it. Only he never did; I mean, it never went beyond a certain point, but all the same, when he said I'd got to give him an alibi, I didn't dream of saying I wouldn't. And I did love him, you see. I wanted to help him if he needed it.'

'Just a minute,' I said, feeling that now that she had started talking it might go on and on. 'You gave him an alibi for the time Mr Loxley was killed.'

She nodded solemnly.

'He told you to?'

She nodded again.

'But I don't understand why,' I went on. 'We're sure it wasn't Fred who killed Mr Loxley, but someone disguised as him, so what was he doing at that time that he should need an alibi?'

I had never felt as unsure that it had not been Fred that I had seen at the gate as I was at that moment.

'I don't know,' she murmured. 'He never told me what he'd been doing. He didn't like being asked how he'd been spending his time. He always had lots of money, so I supposed he worked very hard. But now they're saying he got the money from Mr Bird because he knew something terrible about him. I suppose you think I'm very stupid.'

I nearly said, 'Very simple,' but kept it back.

'How did you hear about his getting money from Mr Bird?' I asked.

'Oh, they're all talking about it down at the Green Man,' she said. 'I think a policeman told someone about Mr Bird saying it, and everyone was saying they'd always believed there was something wrong about Fred, which wasn't true, because he was really very popular.'

'If it's true, it's the reason why he's left you,' I said.

Brian observed, 'He won't get far if he's gone in that red van of his.'

'He'll probably ditch it pretty soon,' Malcolm said, 'and pick up someone else's car.'

'If what he told me is true about the joy-riding in stolen cars,' I said, 'he's probably quite proficient at stealing cars. On the other hand, he may simply have made for the railway.'

'Sharon, if it's any consolation to you to know it,' Malcolm said, his voice very kind, 'he wanted you to know that he had nothing to do with this horrible murder of Lynne Denison. That's why he told you to come to us. He and Mrs Denison were here together in the late afternoon, then she left, and he stayed on, talking to Frances, and he was still here when we were rung up by Jane Kerwood, who told us how Mrs Denison's body had been found. So there are three of us here who know he couldn't have had anything to do with her murder.'

'And you've told that to the police?' she asked.

'Yes.'

She gave a deep sigh. Her tensely folded hands relaxed.

'All the same, I'd like to know what he was doing during that time for which I had to give him an alibi,' she said. 'It's rather peculiar, isn't it? Could he have been meeting Mr Bird to pick up some of the money he was getting from him? I suppose I'll have to tell the police all about it. Will I get into trouble for it, d'you think?'

'You could, if they're feeling nasty,' Malcolm said. 'But if you tell them just the story you've told us, I shouldn't think it will be very serious. If they catch Fred, however, you'll probably have to be a witness at his trial.'

'His trial!' It came out as a little yelp. 'Will there really be a trial?'

'For certain,' Malcolm answered.

She looked at him searchingly, as if she were trying to find some meaning hidden behind what he had said. Then she stood up.

'I mustn't keep you,' she said. 'I only came to ask you about Fred's alibi. It's sad, isn't it, that we'll never do *Romeo and Juliet* now, and we shan't, shall we? I've been learning my lines. "*What devil art thou that dost torment me thus? This torture should be roared in dismal hell, Hath Romeo slain himself?*' . . . Do you think Fred will kill himself? I'd do it myself sooner than let them catch me. Well, goodbye. You've been very kind.'

'I'll drive you down to the old vicarage, if you like,' Malcolm offered.

'Oh no, thank you. It's no distance. Good night.'

We all said good night and Malcolm saw her to the door.

When he came back into the sitting room, I said, 'I'll go to Lucille now.'

'I suppose that's the right thing to do,' he said. 'Come along then. I'll drive you down.'

'I may as well drive myself,' I said. 'I don't know how long I'll be. You might have to sit waiting in the car for an hour or so, because I don't suppose you want to come in to see her yourself – or do you? You can probably give her as much comfort as I can. She might even prefer it.'

'No, I'll leave it to you,' he said.

'Where do you think you'll find her?' Brian asked. 'Will she be in her own home, or will friends have taken her in, as you did Avril?'

'I'll see when I get there,' I said. 'The police will know.'

In fact, she was in her home, sitting stiffly in the small but stately drawing room with Avril and Jane keeping her company, and a tray of coffee on the low table in front of her. The front door was open and a young constable there had doubts about letting me in, but then stood aside so that I could enter, and I went to the drawing room door and asked, 'Shall I come in, Lucille?'

I thought for a moment that she was not going to answer, she simply stared at me bleakly as if she hardly remembered who I was.

Then she said, 'Ah, Frances. Yes, come in. Kind of you to come. You'd like a cup of coffee, wouldn't you? Jane, dear, will you go to the kitchen and fetch a cup for Frances?'

I did not want the coffee, but I did not refuse it. I went forward into the room and sat down on the window-seat. The dark red velvet curtains were drawn, and a log fire was burning in the fireplace. It all looked comfortable and cosy except for the rigidly upright figure of Lucille in the wing-backed armchair beside the fire. I had come intending to say comforting things to her, but now that I was here, I could not think even how to begin.

At last, I said about the most futile thing I could have thought of. 'How are you, Lucille?'

'Just as you would expect,' she answered in her cold voice. 'The reason for my continued existence has gone, but I have always regarded suicide as a sin. To live without a reason, however, is something I have never contem-

140

plated. I have never dreamt it might ever be expected of me.'

Jane returned to the drawing room with the coffee cup for me, poured out coffee and brought it to me.

'Have they taken Kevin away?' I asked.

'Naturally they have,' she said. 'He left them no choice. Meanwhile, of course, I expect to be blamed for the whole catastrophe. An over-possessive mother, that is what I am, and who is more reviled at the present time than the over-possessive mother? She appears to be the origin of all wickedness. It is more acceptable if you let your child run wild and run wild yourself with all the lovers you can acquire so that he shall not be twisted by the terrible burden of your love, than that you should try to use your intelligence and devotion in turning him into a worthwhile member of society. I never thought of myself in my relations with Kevin, you know. The truth is, I was not possessive. He had perfect freedom to do as he liked. If he had brought a wife home to me, I should have welcomed her. Yet do you know, he turned on me tonight with the most extraordinary explosion of hatred. Only a few hours ago, I should never have thought such a thing possible. I did not even know he knew the words he used. It's all most extraordinary.'

Her icy self-control was deadly. I thought it far more abnormal than the wildest hysteria would have been, and wondered what I could possibly say that might at least prick the surface of it, for I did not believe there was any depth to it.

'Of course, you've got him a lawyer,' I said lamely.

'Of course,' she replied. 'Cortwell Denis Dene, my husband's old firm. He was still working for them when he left me, but they've always been very helpful to me and he, of course, has been dead for years. Mr Dene is coming down to see me tomorrow. A very practical, unassuming man, though rather advanced in years. But I do not expect him to be able to help Kevin. Kevin himself will see to it that he does not. It's very strange, but he seems actually to be enjoying his present situation.'

I had not known till then that Lucille's husband had been a lawyer. She had never spoken of him and I had always assumed that the pain of his death had made her unwilling to do so, or perhaps that the marriage had been such a disappointment to her that she preferred not to think about it. That seemed nearer to the truth, and really it explained a good deal about her.

'You're staying on in this house, are you?' I asked.

'Of course,' she said. 'The police have no objection to my doing so.'

'Alone?'

'Certainly.'

'Lucille is very brave,' Jane said.

'Braver than I was,' Avril said. 'Nothing would have got me to spend a night in that house, even with the dogs.'

It occurred to me then for the first time that there was no sign of the dogs in Lucille's house.

'Where have you left them?' I asked Avril. I had a sudden and horrible fear that she had had the poor animals put down, as she had threatened, then realized that it was hardly likely that she could have done so at that time in the evening.

'They're tied up in Jane's garden,' she answered. 'I haven't made up my mind about them. I haven't made up my mind about anything. I feel very stupid compared with Lucille. Here she's been hit by a horror as bad as anything that's hit me, or perhaps worse – yes, I think much worse – and she just makes it plain that she means to go on living her normal life in spite of everything. Jane's right, she *is* very brave.'

'I'm much older than you,' Lucille said, 'that's probably the explanation. Things matter less and less as you get old. The young are very vulnerable. We're always hearing about the vulnerable members of society, women, children and the elderly, and I can't make any sense of it.

Once you're old enough all you really care about is being comfortable. And that, of course, makes money very important. To be old and poor must be very difficult indeed. But I have no worries of that description. I never have had. I always had more money than my husband, and naturally, I've never depended on Kevin in any way. I shall survive.'

I was sure that she would. She was made of steel. If she possessed any emotions, she had them so firmly under control that she had no reason to fear what they might do to her. I began to wonder if what had helped to twist Kevin's nature had not been an excess of mother-love, as I had supposed, but a lack of it. Perhaps he had had an intuition that he was only one of the comforts that she demanded of life. If he had really turned on her in hatred, as she had said, that did not seem unlikely.

We went on talking for some time, but there was evidently nothing that any of us could do for her. After a while, I made the standard remark that if there was anything that I could do for her, she must let me know, and got up to leave. Avril followed my example, then asked me if she could drive home with me, as she had left the things there that she had used the night before. Lucille thanked us in a stately way for coming, and we let ourselves out and got into the car that I had left in front of the house. The evening was very dark by then and a wind had got up. It was much colder than it had been earlier in the day and there was a damp feeling in the air as if it were trying to rain. Some chestnuts on the far side of the road tossed their dark heads against the sky. There was light and noise in the Green Man next door to Lucille's house.

'Oh dear, I've just thought of something,' Avril said as we got into the car. 'When I've collected my things, I'll have to ask if you'd mind driving me down to Jane's, because I don't think I could face walking, I'm so tired.'

'Of course I'll drive you down, or Malcolm will.' I had

just noticed someone come out of the door of the pub; a tall, broad-shouldered man, who turned in the direction of the lane up to our house. 'There's Hugh,' I said. 'Have you seen him today?'

Avril gave a sigh. 'Yes, he called in on Jane and me just before we left to go to Lucille, and Jane, silly creature, ever so tactfully left us alone together and I had the greatest difficulty in stopping him telling me he loved me. I don't believe it, of course. It's Jane he really cares about, but she was always completely wrapped up in Peter, and he only thought of me as a sort of stopgap.'

'So he isn't the father of your child,' I said.

She turned her head to look at me silently. I had started the car and we had already overtaken Hugh.

At last she said, 'No.' There was another silence, then she said, 'I suppose Lynne told you about that. I ought to have known she would. She could never keep anything to herself.'

'Yes, but I'd guessed it already,' I said.

'How did you manage that? It doesn't show yet.'

'Well, in a way it does.'

'How?'

'Oh, I don't know. Something about your face and your suddenly wanting to get rid of the dogs. Are you happy about it, Avril?'

'I don't think I've ever been so miserable in my life.'

'But isn't it what you've always wanted more than anything else?'

'Yes, but not like this. This is all wrong – wrong!'

'Because the father isn't Peter?'

'So Lynne told you about that too.'

'Yes.'

'And are you going to tell everybody about it, including the police?'

'You know I'm not.'

'I suppose I do, yes, you'll stay quiet about it. Poor Peter, he was so hurt and humiliated about it. He hated the dogs, because he took them as a kind of criticism of him, which in a way they were, though that didn't occur to me at the time I got them.'

'Did he know about the child?'

'Oh, yes.' She was silent again, gazing straight before her where the long shafts of light from the headlights cut into the darkness. 'He even knew who the father was. I told him everything.'

'I think I know that too,' I said. 'Isn't he Fred Dyer?'

Avril did not answer. Her silence, as it lengthened out, was as complete an admission that I was right as any answer could ever have been. I left the car in the lane, sure it would be needed immediately to take her down to Jane's, and we walked up to the house together. We found Malcolm and Brian in the sitting room, watching television. Malcolm switched it off as soon as we came in and I explained why Avril had come back with me. She said nothing herself. Silence seemed to have taken possession of her. I went upstairs with her and helped her pack the few things that we had brought over from her house the evening before and went downstairs again. At last, she managed to speak.

'I want to thank you,' she said. 'You've been very kind. I don't know what I'd have done yesterday if you hadn't taken care of me.'

'I'll drive you down to Jane's,' Malcolm said.

'Thank you, that's very kind.' There was a flat monotony in her voice; a sound of hopelessness that made me more sorry for her than I had felt till then.

She and Malcolm set off together down the path to the gate.

'How was Mrs Bird?' Brian asked as I sat down near the fireplace.

'As you'd expect, if you knew her,' I answered. 'Very brave, very proud. She says everyone's going to blame her for having made Kevin what he is. I'm not sure whether or not she thinks so herself. She didn't deny it.'

'Do you think she's known the truth all along?'

'It isn't impossible, but I don't really think so.'

'What will she do now?'

'She'll face it out. She'll stay in that house and if people show signs of avoiding her, or pitying her, she'll look through them as if they didn't exist.'

'You don't think she'll go to those relatives of hers in Canada?'

'I don't think so. She'll want to stay where she can keep some contact with Kevin.'

'He'll get life, of course.'

'Unless he's detained at Her Majesty's pleasure.'

'It doesn't much matter which it is, does it, as long as he's kept very securely out of circulation?'

I leant back in my chair and for a moment closed my eyes. I was aware of a deadly tiredness and a longing to be able to talk about something that was not murder. But there did not seem to be much hope of that for the present.

Brian was going on, 'It's curious how unwilling we all are nowadays to say that a person is mad. We've all sorts of other names for it. Diminished responsibility. Mentally ill. Psychologically disturbed. But we're as unwilling to use the old word, mad, as a lot of people are to talk of death. They prefer to say we only pass over.'

'Like Avril talking of having her dogs put down, not killed. Incidentally, I wonder if she'll really do that.'

I came near to telling him at that moment that Avril would almost certainly get rid of her dogs somehow. To look after them as well as a newborn baby would be somewhat demanding. But I said nothing. My belief that Fred Dyer was the father of the child was quite positive, but I did not feel it was anything that I could talk about, even to Brian. It was to Malcolm that I spoke about it presently, when we had gone up to bed, had switched off the light and had lain side by side in a silence which for some minutes was equally wakeful for both of us.

At last I said, 'She's pregnant, you know.'

148

'Is she?' he said. 'I wondered.'

'What made you do that?' I asked. 'It doesn't show yet.'

'I don't know why I thought of it,' he said. 'It just occurred to me as possible.'

'And it seemed probable that the father's Fred.'

'Is that certain?'

'Not a hundred per cent, I suppose, but I think it's so. When I said to her I thought it was, she just went dead silent. She didn't deny it. And it fits in a number of ways. You know how he used to go into the house for a cup of tea and she said herself they used to gossip over it. Well, I think it might be for more than tea that he went in, because apart from anything else, Lynne told me something rather curious. She told me she offered to lend Avril money if she needed it before probate and all that had gone through, but she was a bit staggered when Avril promptly asked her for ten thousand pounds.'

'I don't think I quite understand the connection,' Malcolm said. 'Are you suggesting that Fred demanded ten thousand pounds for making love to Avril? If so, prostitution must be a more paying occupation than I've ever thought.'

'No, but if Avril thought he and she were going to go away together, she might have needed money quickly. Even if he was blackmailing Kevin, I don't suppose he's got enough put by for the two of them to set off for Australia, which was what he seemed to want to do.'

'And now he's disappeared without his ten thousand pounds. I wonder if Avril knows where he is. It'll be just as well for her if she doesn't, I'd say. He doesn't seem to be an exactly faithful type.'

'I wonder if Peter knew about the child, and if so, whether it had anything to do with his murder. You know, I've a feeling that if we found the right way of looking at it, we'd find it was at the heart of the matter.'

'But with divorce so easy nowadays, it doesn't seem probable.'

'Malcolm, wouldn't it be nice now to go, say, to Spain or Italy.' The itch to talk of something that was not murder had at last become too much for me. 'I've never been to Italy in the spring, when it's supposed to be so wonderful.'

He drew me towards him and kissed me.

'Very nice. But we've got to see this thing through first.'

'We're only involved in it, aren't we, because I saw that man at the gate?'

'Whom you're so sure wasn't Fred.'

'What do you think – could he have been Kevin?'

'Possibly, only it doesn't seem to be Kevin's type of murder. No strangling and black plastic bags. It seems to have been a cold-blooded affair, probably carefully planned.'

'The thing is, Kevin could have had a motive. If Peter had found out the truth about those Edgewater murders, perhaps somehow from Fred, he could have told Kevin he was going to tell the police all about it.'

'Yes, and I suppose there could be two sides to Kevin's nature. Only how could Peter have got the truth out of Fred? It paid him to be the only person who knew it.'

'He could have said something accidentally. Anyway, when this is all over, we're going to Italy.'

'Very well, to Italy. Good night, now.'

'Good night.'

But I believe it was an hour or more before either of us went to sleep.

Next morning, after breakfast, I set out shopping with my shopping trolley. It was a beautiful morning, with clear springtime sunshine brightening the pale green that was growing richer on trees and hedges. It seemed absurd to think too much of what human beings could do to ruin the loveliness of that brief perfection. For of course, it would be brief. It might be raining by the afternoon. There was a flowering cherry in full bloom in the Askews' garden. I found myself thinking about the Askews, wondering why we had not got to know them better and if it was our fault. I thought that perhaps it was a matter of age, that we had felt that it would bore them to spend too much time in the company of people as old as Malcolm and me. But perhaps it was the other way round, that they had thought we would find them a nuisance. I decided I would do my best to rectify the trouble, whatever it was. The fact was, I understand myself well enough to realize that I was craving for contact with people who to the best of my knowledge had no connection with murder.

I went to the village shop, filled my trolley with a number of things, then set off for home. But when I reached Hugh Maskell's gate, I paused, then pushed it open and went up to the house. When I rang, there was a sound of footsteps inside almost immediately and Hugh opened the door.

'Well, this is a pleasant surprise,' he said. 'I thought it might be that man Holroyd. I couldn't think who else it could be. Come in and have some coffee.'

We went into his sitting room where the great window that overlooked the patio was wide open, which made it look as if the strange metal object that might be a nude woman was just about to come walking in.

He hesitated and said, 'I'll shut it, shall I? It's so tempting to have it open on a wonderful morning like this, but it soon gets chilly.'

He closed the window, told me to sit down and said that he would be only a few minutes getting the coffee. I sat down in a chair near the window, and suddenly noticed that on a small table by my side, there was a copy of *Romeo and Juliet*. I picked it up and started leafing through it, finding that it had been liberally annotated in pencil. I was studying it when he returned from the kitchen with two cups of coffee on a tray. I held the book up.

'Are you actually still thinking of going on with this, Hugh?' I asked.

'Perhaps,' he said. 'Later. What do you think about it?'

'It's what I came in to ask you,' I said. 'I've a feeling we ought to keep the dramatic society going, but I can't see us tackling *Romeo and Juliet* now. But we'll have to get back to normal sometime, and something fairly light and cheerful might help to do it. What about something like *The Beaux Stratagem*?'

'Too sophisticated,' Hugh replied. 'Actually much harder to act than Shakespeare. But we must think about it. As soon as it's decent, we must call a meeting of the society and discuss the position. You realize, of course, we've lost three of our male actors. I know Kevin wasn't actually acting in this last show, but he was useful some-times, and of course, the work he put in on designing our sets was invaluable. But that reminds me . . .' He paused, sipping coffee, then gave an embarrassed little laugh. 'This is a nice house, wouldn't you say?'

'Very nice,' I said, taken a little aback by the change of subject. 'I've always liked it.'

'But I'm not sure that I'll be staying on in it. I simply don't know. I can't make up my mind. What do you think, Frances, shall I ever be comfortable living in a house designed by a mass murderer?'

It was a problem that had not occurred to me. One of the reasons why I had come in to talk to Hugh about the problem of the dramatic society, was that it seemed a promising way of escaping from the dread obsession with murder that gripped everyone else I met. But here we were, back to it almost immediately.

'I don't know, perhaps you won't,' I said. 'But you aren't thinking of leaving Raneswood, are you?'

'I'm not sure that I'm thinking of leaving the house,' Hugh said. 'If I can stick it out for the next few months, I might find it developing a sort of legendary quality. People might even come to look at it and want to be shown round it. It wouldn't be exactly like living in a haunted house, but it would be a place with a history.'

'In that case,' I said, 'if it's just the immediate future

that's the problem, why don't you go abroad for a time? That's what Malcolm and I are going to do. As soon as that business in the Magistrates' Court is over and we can get away, we're going to Italy.'

He went to stand at the window, looking out at the metal lady on the patio. A tall, spare figure with broad shoulders, I caught myself thinking. Clap a red wig on his head and gardening gloves on his hands and was it possible . . . ? Just possible . . . ? I began to wish I had not come.

I finished my coffee and stood up. He did not turn, but spoke quietly.

'I've been thinking, you know, that I might be able to bring Avril here and that she would like it. What Kevin did, after all, had nothing to do with Peter's death. At least, I don't think it had. But then I thought that she'd almost certainly want to move much further away, and then I started thinking that perhaps I shouldn't really care about staying on here myself. But suppose she doesn't want me, what do I really want to do?'

'Have you spoken to her yet?' I asked.

'Not really. I tried to, but perhaps naturally, she wouldn't let me. It was a mistake to try.'

'Yes, I'd leave it for the present,' I said, feeling fairly sure that Avril had told him nothing of the child, and that there would be no response from her till she had made up her mind what to do about it. 'Meanwhile, think about our dramatic society and what we can do to keep it going. I'm sure it would be good for us all.'

He saw me to the door, a strangely forlorn figure, it suddenly seemed to me, a very lonely man who just conceivably might do a desperate thing to replace the wife who had died and left him to face an empty life alone.

I dragged my trolley along the lane till I was opposite the Askews' house. Victoria Askew and the two children were in the garden; the children playing some game with a plastic football, and their mother hoeing a bed of wallflowers. On an impulse, I stopped at their gate and waited until she had noticed me. When she saw me, she came quickly to the gate and opened it.

'I've been hoping to see you sometime,' she said. 'You must have been going through a very difficult time. Won't you come in and have some coffee?'

She was about thirty; a tall, slender young woman, with a pale, oval face and gentle brown eyes and dark brown hair brushed back from her forehead and tied in a ponytail with a blue ribbon.

I could have said that I had just been drinking coffee, but something made me accept the invitation. My impulse to stop in the lane when I saw her had been the result of a sudden desire to get to know her better, and to refuse her invitation would not be helpful in doing that. Dragging my trolley after me I followed her up the path to the door. The children paused in their game to stare at me, then started kicking the football again.

She took me into a small, low-ceilinged room with a little bay window with lattice panes and a great fireplace that took up nearly the whole of one wall, on the hearth of which there was still a heap of ashes from a fire of yesterday, or perhaps longer ago than that. The chairs were all covered in what had once been a flowery print, but which with fading and grubbiness had become mostly an indeterminate grey-brown. Books, children's clothes, a pair of Wellingtons and a large dish of fruit, filled up almost all the spare space in the room. But there was an elegant little eighteenth-century table standing in the window on which a glass vase filled with sprays of flowering cherry stood.

'Do sit down – I'll get the coffee in a minute,' she said.

In fact, it took her much longer than a minute, but when it arrived it was real coffee, freshly ground, not the instant coffee that Hugh had given me.

'I suppose your husband's at work,' I said. I knew very

154

little about him except that he was an accountant who belonged to a firm in Otterswell.

'Yes, and I'm sorry he's missed you,' she said. 'We've been wanting to talk to you about something for some time, only the truth is – well, we're a bit shy of doing it. If I talk about it now, will you promise to give me a quite honest answer. I mean, if you think what I'm suggesting is quite absurd, you'll say so. You will, won't you?'

'I'll do my best,' I promised, 'but you make it sound rather formidable.'

'Oh, it isn't formidable at all,' she said. 'I mean, for you. For us it is rather, particularly for Ernest; in fact, if he were here he might not let me talk about it, because he's a very modest person and he'd say I'd no right to trouble you with it. But I'm right, aren't I, you're very involved with the local dramatic society?'

I felt a glow of relief. I had thought that what she had said was going to lead up to murder, that it was going to turn out that she and her husband had some theory about the crimes or some such thing, but after all, it was only our poor old society, which had suffered so desperately during the last few days.

'You want to join,' I said hopefully. 'You couldn't be more welcome.'

'Well, yes,' she said, beginning to twine her fingers nervously together. 'We'd have to do that I suppose, though you wouldn't find that either of us has the least talent for acting. But perhaps you could teach us something about it. No, it isn't quite as simple as that. The fact is, Ernest has written a play and I think it's simply marvellous, and I've been trying to get him to send it to an agent to see if we couldn't do something with it, but when I get round to that he always tells me not to be ridiculous, nobody's going to be interested in it. But I think they would be, I really think they would. It's terribly funny, really good comedy, and it hasn't a big cast and it wouldn't be expensive to produce, which I know is very important nowadays, and it's about quite ordinary people, the kind you meet every day. And so I got the idea . . .' She paused, looking at me diffidently, as if to see if I had already rejected what she was going to suggest.

'You got the idea that our dramatic society might try it out,' I said. 'I think it sounds an excellent idea. You don't know how badly we need a nice piece of comedy to tide us over the next few months. Of course, I can't promise anything, but if you gave it to Hugh Maskell to read, he could tell you if there was a chance of our doing it. I'd like to think we were encouraging local talent. But in case you've never seen any of our productions, I ought to warn you, you might be awfully disappointed in what we made of it. We're very, very amateurish.'

'But you think Mr Maskell wouldn't mind our asking him to read the thing?'

'I'm quite sure of it. If you like, I'll take it round to him myself.'

'Oh, that would be marvellous. I'd like to give it to you now, but I can't really do it without having Ernest's agreement. He's so nervous about showing it to anybody, he might be quite angry with me for doing it. But it'll be all right, will it, if I telephone you this evening, say, or tomorrow, to arrange about giving it to you?'

'Quite all right,' I said. 'But tell me something, there aren't any murders in it, are there?'

'Not one.'

'That's all right then. Just for a minute I was afraid . . . you see, murder's so often made into a comedy nowadays, isn't it, and we couldn't do with that at the moment.'

The door opened and Mrs Henderson came in.

She began to say, 'I'll be going now, Mrs Askew . . .' when she caught sight of me and looked startled.

'I didn't know you was here, Mrs Chance,' she said. 'How are you keeping?'

'About as you'd expect, in the circumstances,' I said. 'Have you come to work for Mrs Askew?'

'That's right, just two mornings a week,' she answered. 'Of course, Mrs Loxley doesn't want me any more, and I need the money. I'll have to find some other work as well, but this is tiding me over, and Mrs Askew really needs the help. I'd do a couple of mornings for you, Mrs Chance, if you'd care for it.'

I could hardly believe my ears. One of the disadvantages of life in Raneswood was that it was almost impossible to get domestic help of any kind and I was really very tired of being tied to a vacuum cleaner, furniture polish, soap powders and all the other necessities of a civilized life. In a few minutes I had arranged that Mrs Henderson should come to me on Tuesdays and Fridays.

She stood looking round the Askews' sitting room with a smile of grim pleasure on her face.

'Of course, I've hardly begun here,' she said, 'but we'll soon put it to rights. About that man we both saw at the gate, Mrs Chance, have they found out yet who he was?'

'Not that I know of,' I said.

'They haven't told you anything about it?'

'Nothing at all.'

'A queer thing, wasn't it, the way we both thought it was Fred Dyer, when it couldn't have been. When you thought about it, his hair was the wrong colour, and then the way he was wearing gloves, and had come up to the house on foot, not in his van, and being so rude to both of us, which Fred Dyer never was. I couldn't say I ever took to him. I always felt there was something wrong about him, but he was never *rude*. All the same, I don't understand why he's disappeared if he wasn't the man at the gate.'

I tried to explain to her about Fred's blackmailing of Kevin Bird, that that in itself was an offence and since it meant that he had kept his knowledge of the Edgewater murders to himself, was a very serious one, but she seemed to find it difficult to take in and lost interest in it.

'Well, good morning, Mrs Askew,' she said. 'I'll be in

again on Thursday. Good morning, Mrs Chance, I'll see you tomorrow.'

She let herself out.

Victoria Askew gave me a crooked little smile.

'It's an ill wind . . .' she said. 'You don't know how hard I've tried to get help since we came to live here. But I don't think I'd ever have gone to the length of committing murder to get it. And I suppose the same could be said of you. But you haven't got two noisy, violent, badly brought-up children to cope with, so your motive isn't quite as strong as mine. They're going to hate it if our house gets tidy. About that man, Fred Dyer . . .'

'Yes?'

'D'you think they'll catch him?'

I did not answer at once. It was because at just that moment my eyes had fallen on a photograph on top of an over-filled bookcase, a photograph of the two Askews, standing side by side, wearing shorts and shirts and holding tennis racquets, and there was no question about it, Ernest Askew was tall and lean and broad-shouldered and given the right clothes and a red wig could have been the man at the gate.

Not that I believed for a moment that he had been. In fact, I took that sudden thought of mine as a warning. I was letting the whole subject become an obsession. I was seeing tall, lean, broad-shouldered men everywhere.

Victoria repeated what she had said. 'Do you think they'll catch him?'

I got to my feet. 'I haven't any idea. I don't know how clever he is. Now, I must be going. And let me know what your husband would like me to do about his play.'

She thanked me warmly as I set off for home.

I tried to convince myself as I went that the play would turn out to be a masterpiece; that without knowing it we had been nursing a genius in Raneswood. Something that was terribly funny, with a small cast and about ordinary people sounded very promising. But the chances that it

158

was anything but very dull and amateurish were actually very small. However, it would be for Hugh to tell the enthusiastic young woman that her husband was no genius. He would do it kindly, but would be firm and explicit. Probably he would judge wisely too. I reached our gate and went up to our door.

As soon as I opened it, I realized that Brian was having yet another of his long conversations on the telephone. That it was a long one I deduced from the way that he was sprawling comfortably in the chair in the hall, beside the telephone. He gave me a smile as I passed him on my way to the kitchen to unpack my trolley, and went on talking, obviously to Judy, because his voice had the peculiarly intimate sound that it always had when he spoke to her. I wondered which of them had rung the other and on whose bill the call would appear. When I had finished my unpacking, I went to the sitting room, where I found Malcolm, drinking sherry. He got some for me and I began to tell him about my visit to Hugh and his doubts about his ability to live contentedly in a house designed by a mass murderer.

'I don't believe I could do it myself,' I said, 'but I should have thought he was tough enough to do it.'

'And it's what he'll probably do,' Malcolm said, 'unless he decides to leave Raneswood altogether. But it might not be easy to sell.'

'It's a nice house,' I said, 'and people have short memories. To someone who didn't actually know Kevin, it probably wouldn't really signify much that he designed it.'

'Frances ... Malcolm ...' It was Brian suddenly coming into the room. 'I've just been having the most extraordinary conversation with Judy. Really extraordinary. Oh, I do wish she'd been here all along, she's so much more astute than I am. She's come up with an astonishing idea. At least, it's astonishing to me, only now I can't think why it never occurred to us at the beginning.

It's about the man at the gate. She's pointed out that it's perfectly possible for a man to disguise himself *as himself.* D'you understand me?'

For a moment I did not, then I saw what he meant.

'You mean the man really was Fred Dyer all the time,' I said.

'Yes, Fred Dyer, disguised so that he couldn't possibly be really himself, in a red wig that just couldn't be mistaken for his own red hair, and wearing gardening gloves, which he normally never did, and arriving on foot instead of in his van, and being careful that you and Mrs Henderson would see him and describe the disguise to the police. Of course, he wasn't expecting you to arrive at just that minute, that was a bonus, because your belief in the disguise carried more weight with the police than Mrs Henderson's alone would have done. It's really so simple once you've thought of it.'

So simple that it looked as if our murder might have been solved on the telephone by a woman in Cheshire.

'But why did he do it, Brian?' Malcolm asked. 'Even if he's the father of Avril's child, I don't believe for a moment he's in love with her.'

'Avril's child?' Brian said in a puzzled way, and I remembered then that though I had told Malcolm all about Avril's pregnancy, Brian still did not know of it. So I told him about it and Malcolm repeated that he did not believe Fred was enough in love with Avril to do murder to get her.

'He did it for money,' I said, suddenly seeing everything very clearly. 'He did it for ten thousand pounds.'

'Isn't that rather a cheap rate as murders go?' Malcolm said.

'He may have realized it was as much as he could get. He wanted to get to Australia and have a bit to set him up when he got there. Ten thousand pounds would be quite useful.'

'Of course, what you're really saying,' Malcolm said, 'is

160

that the person behind the whole thing is Avril. Had you thought of that?'

'Oh yes, I believe I've had a feeling all along that that might somehow be the answer. That alibi of hers in London was just a little too convenient.'

'But why should she want to murder Peter? Divorce isn't a problem nowadays, and actually, she could just have left him. Haven't we talked about that?'

'Money again. I don't think she has any of her own.'

'Well, what are we going to do about it? Tell Judy's inspiration to the police?'

'Of course,' Brian said.

'Let's think about it,' I said. 'I'd rather like to talk to Avril before we do anything, to see if she's got any answers to what we're saying.'

'You don't really think she has, do you?'

'I'd still like to talk it over with her.'

'Well, let's have another drink and go on thinking about it,' Malcolm said.

We'd had our second drinks and some lunch before I set off to have the talk I wanted with Avril. I did not really know what I wanted to talk to her about, but it had something to do with that unborn child of hers. The child, I thought, that probably never would be born, for if we were right that she had arranged with Fred to have Peter murdered, then it seemed likely that she would choose to have an abortion, rather than to have a child when she was in prison.

As I walked down towards Jane's bungalow, I was filled with a disturbing sense of pity, though whether it was for Avril, or for her child, who even if it were to be born into this unhappy world would never know the love of parents, the contentment of home, the companionship of other little ones, I could not have said. I walked on with a stubborn sort of determination, doing my best not to think too carefully of what I intended to say. When I reached Jane's bungalow, I saw the Loxleys' car in the road in front of it, so it appeared that the police had allowed Avril to remove it from the garage. I rang the bell and was greeted by a wild barking of dogs.

I had forgotten about the dogs. They seemed to be loose in the house but I heard no sound of footsteps coming towards the door, so it seemed possible that both Jane and Avril had gone out, perhaps to lunch in the Green Man. But I rang again, and this time I heard lagging footsteps inside and an irritable voice, telling the dogs to be quiet. The door was opened by Avril. The dogs came plunging out at me, sniffing round my ankles, jumping up at me, as if I was a dear old friend of theirs whom they were delighted to welcome. Avril repeated her command that they should be quiet, and gradually they calmed down.

'They're very nervous,' Avril explained. 'They can't understand why they've been brought here.'

She looked very nervous herself, her face pallid and drawn, her hair, usually so smoothly brushed back from her face, hanging loosely on her shoulders. 'Jane's out,' she went on. 'Was it her you wanted, or me?'

'Actually you, Avril, if we can have a quiet talk somewhere,' I said.

'Then come in,' she said, and made the dogs allow me room to pass into the house. 'I think Jane went shopping in Otterswell and won't be back for some time, but in any case, I've got my own two rooms here, where we can be quite private, if that's what you want. It's really a very good arrangement. We get on very well when we meet, but we're quite independent of one another.'

She had led me into a room at the back of the bungalow, with windows that overlooked the stretch of lawn behind it. The room was small but comfortable, simply furnished, with easy chairs covered in a cheerful striped material and light cream curtains. There was something impersonal about it, however, as if Avril had not yet made any impression on it.

'Are we going to talk about something serious?' she

162

asked, with a forced note of cheerfulness in her voice.

'Fairly serious,' I said.

'I was afraid so.' She flung herself down in a chair, gesturing to me to take another and giving an artificial little laugh. 'I could see it in your face as soon as I saw you. Oh God, everything's become so damnably serious, hasn't it? Is it about my baby?'

'Partly.'

'I wish Lynne hadn't told you about it. Soon everyone's going to know all about it, and they'll all be giving me advice about what I ought to do. But I don't want advice. I want a little peace so that I can make up my mind myself. D'you think that's unreasonable?'

'Not if you know all the facts,' I said. 'I've a feeling perhaps you don't.'

There was something wary in the way she looked at me.

'Which facts were those?' she asked, trying to sound facetious.

'That it can almost certainly be proved that Fred Dyer was the man whom I saw at the Loxleys' gate,' I said. 'That he'd disguised himself *as himself*, if you see what I mean. He'd turned himself into an exaggerated version of himself, with that wig that was just too red to be really his hair, and everything else about him being just a bit wrong, so that Mrs Henderson, whom he planned to meet when she was leaving the house should swear it couldn't have been him. Then I came along, and I was ready to say that too. I was sure until this morning that the man couldn't have been Fred. Now I'm sure that it was.'

A look of deep antagonism had replaced the wariness in her eyes. It made her face rather frightening.

'What happened this morning to make you change your mind?' she asked.

'A telephone call from Judy Hewlett, Brian's wife. It was she who pointed out that one can disguise oneself as oneself. And once we'd thought of that, all the other

163

things seemed to fit together. Avril, I haven't come here to frighten you. I felt I ought to warn you. I felt you ought to have some time to think over your position and see if you've any answers to the things you're going to be accused of.'

'Like offering Fred ten thousand pounds if he'd get rid of Peter for me, is that what you mean?' Her voice had gone harsh. 'Is it?'

'That's one of the things,' I said.

'But why should I want to get rid of Peter? You don't know that, do you? Well, I'll tell you. You do know the child couldn't have been his, don't you, but you don't know what he did when he found out about it. Because, as I told you, I told him. Simple little old me, I told him I was going to have a child. And what do you think he did? He said I was to have an abortion, and if I didn't, if I insisted on having the child, he'd kill it. Yes, he said that. He said it'd have a cot death before it was a week old.'

'He didn't mean it,' I said quickly, wondering if I thought so or not.

'Oh yes, he meant it,' she said. 'And he wouldn't give me a divorce, and I was afraid of simply leaving him because I'd no money. And I told all this to Fred and said – oh yes, I did – that I'd give him ten thousand pounds if he'd get rid of Peter for me. And he took me seriously! He thought I meant it! I was only talking nonsense, but he thought I meant it!' She had flung herself back in her chair and let out shriek after shriek of hysterical laughter. 'He thought I meant it and he went and did it. He killed Peter without even telling me he was going to do it. And now I'm going to spend most of the rest of my life in prison.'

I waited until the dreadful laughter had stopped, then I said, 'But you *did* mean it.'

She sat up straight and rigid in her chair, a look of angry astonishment on her face.

I repeated, 'You did mean it.'

'I don't know what you're talking about,' she said. 'What did I mean?'

'That you wanted him to kill Peter. That you asked him to do it.'

'You're mad,' she said. 'As if I could possibly do such a thing. A man I hardly knew.'

'You knew him well enough to have a child by him.'

'That's different. You know it's different.'

'All right, it's different. But it isn't an actual bar to intimacy, however casual it may have been.'

'I tell you, I was only joking. I never meant him to take me seriously.'

'Then how did he get hold of the gun?'

She stared at me with her mouth a little open.

'The gun?' she said.

'Peter's gun, with which Peter was shot. How did Fred get hold of it if you didn't give it to him?'

She went on staring at me, saying nothing, but a change came about in her face. A wildness that I suddenly found extremely alarming and that made her eyes brilliant. I felt for a moment that she was going to hurl herself at me and I tensed myself to resist it. But I was wrong, which was fortunate for me, for she was young and powerful and I was elderly and not notably strong. Instead, she leapt to the door, shot through it and slammed it behind her. I heard the key turn in the lock. Then, while the dogs broke into a frenzy of barking, I heard the slam of the front door and a moment later the sound of a car starting. By the time I had climbed out of the window into the garden, gone round the bungalow and reached the road, the Loxleys' car had disappeared.

I stood there, bewildered, wondering where she could be going. Then it occurred to me that perhaps she did not know herself and I began to think what a fool I had been to come and try to talk to her. Because of our past friendship I had wanted somehow to help her and all I had done was frighten her out of her wits. If I had had any sense, I would have got Malcolm and Brian to go to Detective Inspector Holroyd with me and tell him what we had made of Peter's murder. Feeling extraordinarily annoyed with myself, I started for home and as I turned into the lane that led up to our house was suddenly shocked to see that there was a police car at our gate.

The inspector had got there before me. With his great bulk and his strange pixie face, with the eyebrows that tilted up at the ends, he managed to make our sitting room look cramped and somehow commonplace. Malcolm and Brian were also there.

The inspector stood up as I came in, and said, 'Good afternoon, Mrs Chance. I believe you've been visiting Mrs Loxley.'

'I have,' I said, 'and I've got to apologize for what I've done. I've frightened her into making a bolt for it. I don't know where she's gone, but she's left Raneswood.'

'Of course, it was to be expected she'd do that once she knew that we'd identified Dyer as the man you saw at the gate. I came to tell you that we'd some fairly definite evidence that that's who he was, and I wanted to know if in spite of that you still stuck to it that he was someone disguised as Dyer. Now your husband and Mr Hewlett have told me that you'd all come to the conclusion that he was Dyer disguised as himself. That fits very conveniently with the evidence we've got.'

'May I know what that evidence is?' I asked.

'It's a matter of two red hairs inside the red wig from your dramatic store,' he said. 'Hairs that match exactly some red hairs we found in the flat of Sharon Sawyer, which are indisputably Dyer's. In other words, it's clear that Dyer had that wig on his head at some time or other. So it seemed fairly certain that in spite of your doubts, he'd been the man at the gate, even though we didn't yet know what his motive might have been.'

I turned to Malcolm.

'Have you told the inspector about Avril's pregnancy?' I asked.

'Yes, and that Dyer almost certainly committed the murder for the money she'd promised him.'

'But there's something more you should know about her motive,' I said. 'She told me that she'd told Peter about the child, and that he'd insisted on an abortion, and if she wouldn't have one, he said that he'd kill the child. I think that fact might help her when it comes to her trial.'

But it never came to a trial. Where Avril was thinking of driving no one will ever know, but she got on to the M5 and appeared to be heading for Scotland. She was not known to have any friends or relatives in Scotland, but she was driving in that direction at nearly ninety miles an hour when a police car picked her up and gave chase. It made her try to increase her speed and in passing one of those great lorries that lumber along the motorways, she lost control and plunged into the side of the lorry. It rolled over sideways on top of the car, which burst into flames. By the time that the police car arrived, both Avril and the child that was never to be born were dead.

Was it intentional? It is a comfort to me to think so, because I have to face the fact that I was partly responsible for what happened, and it is a help to think that she would have chosen the end that came to her rather than endure the years in prison of which she had spoken to me. For certainly she would have been sentenced. When Fred Dyer was caught in Northern Ireland, he talked without restraint, confirming that Avril had offered him ten thousand pounds to get rid of her husband for her. If the plot had succeeded, she would have inherited all Peter's money and have been able to let people assume that the child was his. Perhaps she had not thought of the fact that she would be subject to blackmail by Dyer, though he would have been at her mercy too. If he had gone to Australia or any other far off place and made a success of his life there, they would probably both have been satisfied to put their crime behind them.

As soon as the inquest on Peter was over, Brian returned to Granborough, where Judy joined him. Fred Dyer at the time had not yet been caught. It was some weeks before that happened and before it did, Malcolm and I set off for a visit to Italy. We stayed for a good deal longer than we had intended, and much that went on in Raneswood was only communicated to us by post, most of it by Jane. For instance, it was she who wrote to tell us that she and Hugh Maskell had decided to get married. They were going to live in her bungalow and put Hugh's house up for sale. It remained empty for some months, but was eventually bought by a retired professor of psychology, who traced the artist who had created the figure of a woman in the patio and commissioned him to produce another, only noticeably male. When we returned to Raneswood, we found him and his wife interesting and friendly neighbours.

Jane found good homes for the three dogs, actually keeping the Belgian shepherd for herself. I do not know how much disturbed the dogs were at being separated, but at least they were not put down. The Loxleys' house has remained empty to the present time. It is a very pleasant house, but with the housing market what it is, buyers had not plunged into buying a house where murder had been committed. A solicitor in London is responsible for it and has contracted with a firm in Otterswell to keep the garden in order. From time to time, the windows get broken by vandals, but eventually, I suppose, someone will decide that it is his or her dream house and the story of the murder will fade into a half-forgotten legend.

After all, how many people know anything much about their predecessors in the houses in which they live contentedly? Malcolm and I know nothing about the people who lived in our house before us. We bought it from a young couple who were moving to a cottage on the island of Barra. We knew nothing about why they wanted to go to Barra, or what happened to them once they were in their cottage there, and no one ever told us about who had lived in our house before them. For all we know, murder was done there. Perhaps if we took seriously the job of digging up our whole garden, we should come on a part of it where a number of bodies are buried. I admit it is unlikely, but it is not impossible. Our experiences during that spring in Raneswood have left me with a feeling that very few things are impossible.

Lucille remained in her home in Raneswood. Except that she became even more proud and stiff and unapproachable than before, there was very little change in her. No one dared to express any pity for her. She went on playing bridge and occasionally asking neighbours in for drinks, and it somehow became recognized in the village that she held herself responsible for all that her son had done, although this did not mean that she was to blame for it. As was only to be expected, he was detained at Her Majesty's pleasure. It is to be hoped, I think, that this will last for as long as his life, and that he will not be returned to be cared for in the community. Not that Lucille would shrink from undertaking this, but after all, she is much older than he is, and a time would probably come when he would be left alone to commit what further murders he chose. Malcolm and I have discussed his case with our new neighbour, the professor of psychology, who is very sure that the Kevins of this world should be kept shut away. 'The well should be protected from the sick,' he says, an attitude which is not as popular these days as I think it ought to be.

Just how sick Avril Loxley was will never be ascertained, or Peter either, for that matter. If she told me the truth that he had threatened to kill her child if she insisted on letting it be born, perhaps he was the sicker of the two. But those are problems to which there are no answers.

Ernest Askew was persuaded by his wife to submit the play that he had written to Hugh Maskell, and Hugh, most reluctant to look at it at first, fearing to be put into the embarrassing position of having to tell the writer that it was a piece of amateurish blundering, was overcome with pleasure at finding it just what Victoria Askew had said, exceedingly funny and splendid entertainment. The dramatic society made it their Christmas production and it was an amazing success. It happened that an agent from London was in the village, staying with friends, and was taken to see it, and now there are rumours going round that it will be produced in London sometime next year. In fact, without anyone suspecting it, we have had a village Chekov living amongst us. I was in our local production, as an elderly lady who spends most of her time throughout the play playing patience and had only about three lines to say. I enjoyed it very much.

Sharon Sawyer, as shyly and diffidently as ever, soon acquired another boyfriend. Gossip had it that he treated her as badly as it seemed she liked to be treated. He was part owner of a small market garden in the neighbourhood.

Malcolm is still writing his autobiography, but cannot make up his mind what treatment he should give to his experiences of murder. I believe he is tempted to leave them out altogether.